CHAPTER 1

"...Life is like a box of chocolates. You never know what you're gonna get." I heard Forrest say through the television as I sat Indian-style on my mother's bedroom floor eating popcorn while watching the Forrest Gump movie on VHS. It was the summer of '96, and I was only eight years old. My birthday was in a couple of months and I couldn't wait.

My older cousins, Vell and D-Bo, would always shower me with the finer things in life. Everything that my mom couldn't afford, they got it for me. Unbeknownst to me my mom was a crack smoker, and at the time I was too young to recognize the traits. I didn't really know what a crack smoker looked like, even though my friends and I thought we did. Everybody that was dirty looking or homeless was considered a crackhead to us.

When somebody came to school dirty, we would sing, "Ya momma's on crack rock!" Me not knowing the entire time that my mom was on it harder than Marion Barry in Colombia.

Vell and D-Bo kept me fresh, so who would suspect that my mother was an addict? I was my mom's only child so it was easy for my cousins to look after me. At least until...

"POW! POW! POW! POW! POW!"

Immediately afterwards I heard a car door slam at the same time I heard a female's voice scream and then, "BLOCKA! BLOCKA! BLOCKA! BLOCKA! BLOCKA! BLOCKA! BLOCKA!" Screeching tires ended the episode.

Seconds later my mom came bursting through her room door, breezing past me and rushing directly towards her bedroom window to look outside. "Oh my god," she said to herself, as she turned around to look at me, her left hand covering her mouth as if she was trying to hold something in. "Louie! Go to your room and get ready for bed," Momma said, her voice wavering nervously. She walked over to the TV and pressed the power buttons, turning off the television and video tape player. I slowly stood up with my bowl of popcorn in hand, looking as confused as I was at the time. My mom then snapped her head in my direction, giving me an angry stare before pointing toward the bedroom door and yelling, "GO!"

I immediately dropped the popcorn bowl and damn near left behind my socks as I ran out of her bedroom faster than Wild E Coyote shooting out of a cannon. Once I was in my bedroom I could hear the sirens of an ambulance, police cars and fire trucks outside my window while I changed into my G.I. Joe pajamas. When I was finished getting dressed, I climbed from my bed onto my clothes cabinet to peak through the blinds covering my window. Momma had positioned my clothes cabinet in front of my window because we lived in a violent neighborhood. Stray bullets could fly through a window on any given day with no name issued to them so that cabinet was like my shield, even though at the time I didn't understand. I just thought it was there so that I couldn't look outside when I was on punishment.

"Get your ass out of that window and into bed, boy!" Momma yelled once again, scaring the hell out of me. Momma stood in the doorway with her right hand on her hip. I didn't even hear her coming. I thought I was about to shit on myself as I dove into my bed and yanked my blanket over my head.

"Don't let me come back and catch your yellow ass in that window again!" Momma said with emphasis as she closed my bedroom door.

I laid under my blanket listening to all of the screaming and hollering going on outside of my bedroom window and bedroom door. It felt like an hour had passed before I heard my big cousin DaVell walk into our house talking loud as hell about how he was going to kill somebody. No more than ten minutes later, while I was fading into my thought, I heard Vell outside of my bedroom door talking on the phone to someone saying, "Germ and 'em gotta go." There was a pause before I heard him again, "You take one of mine... I take all of yours."

Whoever Germ was, I felt sorry for him and his. Everybody knew my cousins Vell and D-Bo. Vell was the older of the two. He stood about six foot even and was 185 pounds solid. He had light skin and curly hair. Vell and D-Bo's father was Puerto Rican and a pro boxer. He died a couple of years ago in a motorcycle accident but because of their father, Vell was pretty good with his hands.

Vell was a go-getter. A hell of a hustler, with endless respect, money, women and power. D-Bo on the other hand was no more than two inches shorter than Vell, but had to be an intimidating 200 pounds solid. He too had a light complexion, with long curly hair in which he kept corn rolled. His hair stretched past his shoulders to the middle of his back. Though D-Bo was the younger of the two, he was feared the most because of his constant aggression in the streets. D-Bo was well known for squeezing the trigger, robbing dope boys and packing some of the best hands on our side of town. A well-known knock-out artist.

I loved my cousins for a lot of reasons, but the main reason was because of how they treated me more-so as a little brother. I have to admit, D-Bo was my favorite out of the two because of the quality time that he spent with me. He was the one who taught me how to fight and he once made a girlfriend of his suck my pecker when I was five years young. I'm sure Vell would have spent a lot more time with me if he wasn't the bread winner of the family. We all survived because of him, and even my mom didn't know what we would do without the two of them.

After about another twenty minutes of thinking about the Forrest Gump movie and how I was eager to watch the rest tomorrow, that quote, "...Life is like a box of chocolate, you never know what you gonna get," played over and over in my head as I faded into a deep sleep. Little did I know that quote was going to be the slogan of my life.

CHAPTER 2

Fast forward to 2014, and everything in my life changed. Everything about life itself had changed. Tupac and Biggie Smalls had since been murdered; Michael Jordan had won his sixth NBA Championship before retiring in a legendary fashion. He even, once again, returned to the NBA from retirement and signed with my Washington Wizards, who changed their name from the Bullets. Now who would've thought that would happen? Go figure.

Before that, we found out that white presidents smoke weed and get head. Sounds like a black man to me. The United States of America even suffered a vicious tragedy on my 14th birthday, September 11, 2001.

Ricky Williams and a cast of other pro players traded football in to smoke weed, and to most likely get some head, too. Phil Jackson proved why he is arguably the best NBA head coach of all time by winning 11 championships. LeBron James showed us why he's respectively not the greatest basketball player, by losing three out of five. And we finally got what we've been looking for all of these years. A black President of the United States; one who even admitted to smoking weed at least once. And I'm pretty sure he was getting some presidential knowledge in the process.

Another crack law passed, which would release 50,000 federal inmates by November of 2015. Go black president!

Marijuana was medically cleared in most states, for recreational use in a few others and decriminalized in some states also, including my home, Washington D.C. A lot of things have changed in 18 years but some things never do, such as the Washington Redskins. They still hadn't gotten it together. Maybe they need a brand new identity.

Another thing that hadn't changed was racial profiling. From Florida to Missouri, New York to California. Some things will never change. Maybe America needs a new identity.

It seems as though since my cousin D-Bo got murdered outside of my apartment building that night, my entire family grew a new identity. Nothing was the same. I was raised in Paradise Apartment Complex in the Northeast section of DC.

Our apartment complex was connected to another neighborhood called Mayfair Mansion Apartments. The two hoods are connected with no thru streets in a design of a race track, because that's what it once used to be many years ago before my existence.

There was a giant one way street that ran on the outside of the two neighborhoods in a shape similar to a horse shoe. Mayfair has a six foot black gate around its premises while Paradise has a five foot green gate. The buildings are sectioned off into courts in both neighborhoods, but unlike Mayfair, Paradise courts were named to distinguish them. Their courts were named Miracle, Faith, Freedom, Unity, Courage, Harmony and Justice.

Growing up there, you had to be tough. If you didn't know how to fight, you'd learn. If you didn't know how to hustle, shoot a gun or use a condom, you would definitely learn. There had to be somewhere between three to five thousand residents that lived amongst the two hoods. It was a busy area. You would often hear Go-Go bands shout out our hoods, saying slogans like, "Mayfair Don't Play Fair" or, "Paradise Got That Ice". And somehow, somewhere, "Cruddy Island" recently became the perfect name that represented the two neighborhoods, because that's exactly what it was. Everybody was snaking each other out for the love of the mighty dollar. Loyalty was just a word for the dictionary, and love was made for your mother only.

By now you should have gotten the picture... it was rough. I was protected by that cabinet in my bedroom until I was about 14 years old. After that, it was time for me to find my own way. Momma had stopped using crack about two years after D-Bo was murdered and she dedicated her life to God. So when I started selling crack at 13, and momma found out, she told me that I had a year to find a new residence.

The hustler mentality was forefront in my mental breakdown and so I naturally started stacking my cash, met a bad chick and together we rented out some old man's two bedroom, one bath apartment on Dubois Place in Southeast DC. My lady, Tanya, who is now my son's mother, is two years my senior. She attended day and night school at Spingarn Senior High School in Northeast, which helped her graduate school at the early age of 16. Immediately afterwards, she started dancing at strip clubs while taking college courses at Prince Georges Community College in Largo, Maryland.

Together she and I saved up a nice amount of cash; enough to place a down payment on a house, but we decided against the idea of buying and settled for an apartment inside a high-rise building called Golden Rule in Northwest, DC. The two bedroom, full bathroom condo-style apartment had a balcony and view of the city's bright lights. It was a beautiful fit for my family.

The only problem about the building was the huge female population. Here I am standing six foot three inches tall, with a light tan complexion. I was tattooed like the subway in Harlem, with wavy hair spinning off my temple taper and a fade in the back. Tanya knew these females were going to try me. It's like she was testing my will power. It was an old fashioned, Boston George set-up.

It was a trap from the start, but it wasn't an issue. I don't creep where I sleep anyway. I'm a hustler and I don't need any extra problems drawing heat to myself, especially around my home. Tanya was enough. Then came my son, Louis Darnell Bigsby. I chose his middle name after my cousin, D-Bo. He was born October 27, 2004, the last day that I sold crack.

CHAPTER 3

Francis Bacon said, "He that hath a wife and children hath given hostages to fortune." Well, I guess it's time to pay the ransom. After Tanya gave birth to my son, I nicknamed him Little Bo. My mom was at the hospital when my son was born. It meant a lot to me to have her support.

Little Bo was born at George Washington Hospital in Northwest. A couple of hours after his birth, my mom and I took a walk to Georgetown, just minutes away, to get us something to eat and also to vent our happiness and thoughts to each other while Tanya's family and friends showed their love and support and welcomed Little Bo. After about a 20-30 minute stroll, we decided to settle in and eat at a nice restaurant on the waterfront called Tony & Joe's.

The food was perfect. My mom is a beautiful chocolate skin toned woman. When she stopped using drugs you could really see the quality of her beauty and features. My mom has long, thick black hair that stretches to the small of her back with beautiful gray streaks displaying all of the hell she experienced in life. Five feet, seven inches tall with a petite build, my mom was a head turner. My sperm donor was a one night stand my mother met at a house party. Momma said she ran into him when she was three months pregnant and informed him that he was the father. She said, from the look on his face, she knew that would be the last time she would hear from him. My mom is a strong woman so she just charged it to the game and raised me alone.

My mom and I discussed how I needed to change my life for the sake of my son. She also explained to me something I'd been wondering since 1996. Why D-Bo was murdered. She explained to me how Vell kept D-Bo sheltered and away from the drug business and would never allow him to sell drugs. She told me that Vell tried his best to supply D-Bo with all of his material wants and needs to ease D-Bo's temptations of hustling, but D-Bo was his own man and was determined to place himself in the game, disobeying Vell's wishes.

That's when D-Bo decided to rob a well-known hustler named Shawn Frye from the Lincoln Heights projects also in Northeast. Shawn Frye went by the nickname "French Fry" because his mom was from Paris. French Fry placed a $50,000 dollar bounty on my cousin, D-Bo. D-Bo had robbed French Fry for three kilos of powder cocaine. French Fry's right hand man, a known shooter named Germaine AKA Germ, took the hit. D-Bo was living with my mom and me at the time of his death, and it was no secret to anybody in Northeast who knew or heard of D-Bo that D-Bo wasn't ducking nothing and nobody.

A lot of people used to think that the letter "D" in his name stood for Drama. Germ sat in a car outside of our apartment building in the parking lot, patiently waiting for D-Bo's arrival. My mom said that D-Bo and his potentially pregnant girlfriend, Stacy, rode a taxi cab to our house that night. She said that as soon as D-Bo and Stacy got out of the taxi, Germ rose up out of his car and in front of about ten people, fatally shot D-Bo and wounded Stacy with two bullets in the process.

Mom said that Germ then hopped back into his car and quickly pulled out of the parking lot but not before his car was shot at. Germ was hit once in the shoulder by a neighborhood hustler named Monkey Seed.

Though D-Bo and Vell weren't originally from my neighborhood, everybody knew who they were and respected them as well as the rest of my family. Stacy cooperated with the police in identifying Germ as the shooter. Germ pled guilty to a 20 years to life sentence. That was the last time that our family heard from Stacy.

Word on the streets was that she was in a witness protection program somewhere in Colorado. My mom said that D-Bo murdered French Fry's little brother, Manny, who was inside their home at the time D-Bo had robbed them. She also told me that French Fry was murdered about two months after D-Bo's death. In a six month span, 14 people were murdered in Northeast alone. My cousin Vell, then pled to a three year sentence for involuntary manslaughter.

An armed and masked man was climbing through his dining room window before Vell stabbed him to death with a kitchen knife. Even though Vell immediately reported the incident to the police, he was still charged and convicted. Vell's attorney tried his hardest to file motions to have the case dismissed, arguing that it was a justifiable homicide.

The government didn't want to hear that. At sentencing, the judge said to Vell, "Next time Mr. Braxton, I expect you to go about this smarter. Go secure yourself in a room and call the police."

Mom said that Vell's response was, "Next time your honor, I will act wiser, and not call the police at all."

That was in 1997. Vell was released on parole in the year 2000.

Vell was sitting comfortably on a nice piece of change, so he left the

drug game behind and opened a boxing gym as well as a tow truck

service. Big cuzo was 100% legit.

I had promised my mother that I wouldn't sell crack again but I

never said that I wouldn't sell drugs again.

CHAPTER 4

I decided to downgrade a little. Between Tanya and me, we had saved a little over 100 grand in our three years of hustling. I humbly sat on my cash for about three months before deciding what needed to be done. After discussing my decisions with Tanya, she agreed and volunteered her services. I was now officially the weed and x-man. Tanya hollered at her co-worker and friend, Sandy, who danced with her at the strip club about a connect.

A couple of days later, Tanya gave me some dude named Jay's number. Jay was from Charlotte, North Carolina. Jay was the father of Sandy's two year old daughter. After about a three or four minute conversation with Jay, we agreed upon meeting up the next week at Bazz and Crue, a strip club in Forestville, Maryland. At that time, that was where Tanya and Sandy worked. I met with Jay and learned a lot about him outside of the business at hand. At the time, Jay was eighteen years young.

He was a light skinned dude with black wavy hair, had a height of about 5'10 inches and carried around about 200 pounds of weight. He let me know that he'd spent most of his juvenile life as a stick-up kid, which his cautious demeanor confirmed. Plies said it best, "How you gonna rob a robber!?"

He also let me know that he was from a neighborhood called Wingate Apartments on the West Boulevard on the west side of Charlotte.

After about two hours of conversation and filling each other out, we finally orchestrated a deal and later that week made a transaction. I was now grabbing and moving 50 pounds of some mid-grade Mary Jane at $400 per pound. After about six months of that, I started purchasing 20 pounds of loud at $2500 a pound in addition to the 50 pounds of regular.

Later, I then stumbled across a connect for the ecstasy pills at one dollar a pill from a dude named Lil Marty from West Baltimore. At the time, Lil Marty was seventeen years young. He stood about 5'6 inches tall, 150 pounds. He was a slick talking, smooth and advanced young cat. He was dark skinned with dreads and had a distinct sounding voice. He told me that he was a rapper and went by the name Boxcheckk Marty. In a way, he kind of resembled Lil Wayne.

One day, I drove up to Bazz and Crue on some chill shit, and Sandy approached me to let me know that Lil Marty was someone she was dealing with and that he was looking for a half pound of loud. She had also let me know that he had the e-pills on deck.

He and I shared conversation for roughly ten minutes and that was enough to let me know that he was official. Nothing about slim said police. He had great eye contact with a solid delivery and a choice of words that only another street smart soldier could understand.

The next day we met in the parking lot of Dave & Busters at Arundel Mills Mall in Anne Arundel County, Maryland. I gave him half a pound for $1800 and he sold me 5000 pills for a dollar a piece. He went home with $3200 in his pocket, and I left with a smile big enough for a toothpaste commercial. It was the start of a beautiful relationship.

In 2010, I caught a gun case around my hood for a ten shot, P-89 Ruger in which I was acquitted, thanks to God and my attorney, Stephen Cooper. I ended up catching another gun case in 2012 in Landover, Maryland in which I plead to one year probation for a misdemeanor charge, to carrying a pistol without a license. It was a throwback, nine shot .22 caliber revolver. At that time, I also had a 33 shot M-1 assault rifle in a duffel bag, but immediately dropped the bag and distanced myself from it at the sight of the cops. I was walking into my cousin's apartment building on Nalley Road. At my preliminary hearing, the officers stated that they never saw the duffel bag in my possession so Mr. Cooper showed the government a sample of how he would destroy their allegations in trial. They then offered me a misdemeanor plea to just the revolver, which was on my waist line at the time of arrest. I took that one on the chin.

Mr. Cooper was a great attorney. He had a strong team of investigators that played a major part in making cases disappear like a skinny woman in a fat girl's club. I definitely got my money's worth. I felt as if I was on top of my game in the streets and had the money, power and the respect to prove it.

I wasn't no big time coke dealer or heroin hustler, but I made a hell-of-a living selling weed, loud, and e-pills. I was purchasing 50 pounds of mid-grade at $400 per pound and letting it fly for $600 a pound. Now, I'm purchasing 25 pounds of loud at $2200 a pound and letting them go from anywhere between $1800 to $2200 a half and between $3000 to $3500 a pound, depending on the quality of the customer and the quantity of the purchase. I'm also selling e-pills at two dollars a pill, no less than 100 pills at a time.

I'm doing me to the fullest. I also rented out another apartment at Carriage Hill Apartments, a complex in Temple Hills, Maryland in which I was using to stash my work inside. I then bought a low key, gray 2008 Kia Sorrento utility truck which I used as my money maker on wheels. I also purchased a 2012 Mercedes-Benz CLS63 AMG. Black on black, and beautiful enough for Tanya and Little Bo to look good in.

The Benz is in Tanya's name since she's currently a case worker at Prince George's County Detention Center in Upper Marlboro, Maryland. Tanya has been working that job for the past eight years. She quit dancing at clubs in 2005 after Little Bo was born. She then transferred from Prince George's Community College to Strayer University in which she studied and received a Bachelor's Degree in 2006 for Public Relations. So the only time I get to drive the Benz is on special occasions like next week, for my birthday. The birthday that re-routed my life in a mysterious way for the better.

CHAPTER 5

"Stopping while you're ahead is not the same as quitting..." was the last thing that I heard before pressing the power buttons, turning off the TV and DVD player. I was watching American Gangster while getting dressed and ready to go out and eat for my birthday celebration. This year my birthday landed on a Thursday, so mom dukes and Tanya decided to take me out to eat. After putting on my black Columbia windbreaker jacket, my cell phone rung.

"What's up, who dis?" I asked, answering my phone.

"What's up bruh, this Rambo." The voice on other end of the line responded. Rambo was originally from 21st Street, also in Northeast, but hung around Cruddy Island, especially after having a baby by my partner Coogi's little cousin, Honesty. Rambo was a thorough young dude that loved to bust that pistol at a high rate.

"Ram, what's up wit'cha slim?" I asked, excited to hear from him.

"Ain't shit, just trying to see if you could go in the studio and turn the volume up on this track a notch? I can barely hear my adlibs, bruh." Rambo said.

"Aight, you want me to fix the whole song or just a certain part?"

"The whole thing, bruh. Just turn it up one notch, that's all." Rambo said.

"Aight, that's a bet then. I got you later. Right now I'm on my way out to eat with the family for my b-day, but I gotta swing through that side of town to drop off mom dukes later on. After I do that I'ma call your phone and see where you at." I said.

"Aight, that's a bet bruh. Don't forget a nigga, bruh. I need that ASAP, bruh."

"On Murda Team, I got you slim." I replied before ending our call. After Rambo informed me that he wanted to upgrade his purchase to a whole thing, I then grabbed a pound of loud pack, placed it into my black gym bag and then let Tanya and the crew know that I was ready to go and to meet me outside in the car.

On my way out, I grabbed the trash bag out of the trash can in the kitchen and walked out of the door ahead of my family. As soon as I got outside in the parking lot, I placed the gym bag inside of the trunk of my Benz, before tossing the trash bag into the large green dumpster can that is stationed in the parking lot.

While climbing into the Benz driver seat, I looked towards our building door, and saw my three favorite people in the world walking out of the door, ready to eat. We went to eat at KOBE Japanese Steakhouse in Largo Town Center in Largo, Maryland. Just me, Tanya, mom dukes and of course, Little Bo.

I slid the hostess a $50 dollar bill to make sure we were all seated together. KOBE is an upscale Asian restaurant that doesn't mind seating you with a complete stranger. It was my birthday, and I wanted to eat with my family or we would have to go elsewhere. After we ate, I first drove mom home while Little Bo snored the entire ride in the backseat, as if he had himself a nine-to-five. Little Bo had slobber everywhere at one point.

I thought Sony PlayStation had some type of spell on my son because as soon as we pulled into our parking lot, he immediately woke up woozy as hell, saying, "Where my game at?"

I looked into my rearview mirror at Little Bo as I was parking while Tanya turned around in her seat to look back at Little Bo with her mouth wide open in surprise.

Tanya and I then turned and looked at each other before simultaneously bursting into laughter, as we shook our heads from left to right in shame. "That don't make no damn sense." Tanya said, as I placed the car into park. After turning off the car, we got out and I had to pick Little Bo up in my arms because he was sleep walking, looking like he was drunk at the bar.

As soon as we got inside the house, he ran straight to his room and powered up his PS4. All I could do was shake my head. I then got myself into the shower to get clean and as soon as I walked out of the bathroom, Tanya went inside to shower herself also. After getting myself together, I walked into Little Bo's room to see him sitting on his bedroom floor with his game controller in his hand, slumped over with his chin in his chest, asleep.

I turned off his TV and game system before prepping Little Bo for bed. He was out for the rest of the night. When I walked into my bedroom, Tanya was already out of the shower walking towards me from out bed with just her towel wrapped around her body like a halter top mini skirt. I had on some silk Polo boxer shorts and a tank top tee. Tanya placed both of her hands on my chest and kissed me, as she guided me to the bed, before pushing me onto it rear-end first.

My backside flopped onto the bed as Tanya dropped her towel to the floor. She then walked her sexy ass over toward the bedroom door, closing and locking it. Tanya was three times sexier from when I first met her. And it seemed as if her birthing Little Bo only made her body find its full potential. A mare indeed. With caramel skin and those seductive eyes, a lot of people compared her to Keri Hilson. Tanya had a flat, smooth stomach and stood five-foot seven inches tall, with a perfect set of breasts and a nice round ass. She had a shape like Eve, just with a little more breast.

Tanya kept her hair cut low with a curly top and a golden brownish color that complemented her complexion. She also wore a tattoo of a tiger on the left side of her body starting from her left breast, wrapping around her rib cage, left butt cheek and all the way down and around her left thigh, with the tail wrapping around her left leg.

Tanya eased her way over to me and placed her palms on my thighs before slowly easing down to her knees, grabbing at my boxers and aggressively yanking them down past my knee caps to my ankles. Seductively looking into my eyes, Tanya whispered, "Sit back and chill, I got him."

So I laid back as Tanya slowly kissed and licked up my inner thigh while gently caressing my genitals with one of her hands before inserting it into her mouth. After about 20 seconds of sucking, she then kissed from the bottom of my penis to the top with no hands.

When she finally reached the top of my bell head, she then slurped just the head inside her mouth. At that point, it felt as if Tanya had an extra tongue. She sucked and slurped just the head for at least two strong minutes, before in one motion, deep throating the whole thing.

My toes then curled as my abs tightened, while I removed my feet from the boxer shorts that were around my ankles. With every stroke, Tanya deep throated with no gag reflex, making my eyes roll to the back of my head like the Undertaker himself.

Every time that I reached for her head, her hands aggressively grabbed my wrist and pinned them to the bed. At this point, I was moaning with oohs and ahhs, sounding like a bitch. I was starting to think she had three tongues now. I even thought I heard myself say, "Marry me."

After about ten minutes of Tanya's oral pleasure, I was ready to let my volcano erupt.

"I'm cumming." I whispered to Tanya, triggering her to suck with more energy. It seemed like the faster she sucked the wetter her mouth became. In a matter of seconds, my unborn children were playing freeze tag in Tanya's mouth.

She sucked every seed out of me. It was like a snake bit my dick and she had to suck the poison out before I died.

As soon as she popped my dick out of her mouth, she swallowed with not a drip coming out. Tanya then seductively climbed her body on top of mine, placing her right hand on my chest while guiding my dick into her perfectly shaved pink pussy with her left.

She then rode me like a wild bull. I swear Tanya's sex had improved 100% throughout time. I guess them drunk machine bull rides at Cadillac Ranch paid off. Tanya rode me for roughly ten straight minutes while I aggressively grabbed at her waist and ass cheeks, stroking her from beneath. I then got tired of her successfully dominating me, and then flipped her over to a missionary position, pinning her legs onto my shoulders and long stroked the juices out of her pussy. It was time for me to show my bossy ways.

Tanya was moaning about something in her stomach at the same time that her hands were reaching for the blankets, in search of something to grip. I held the back of her knee caps, pinning her legs upwards with my hands as I stood up looking down at my dick as I stroked in and out of her pretty pussy.

"I'm 'bout- I'm 'bout – cu – cu- cuuum, baby!" Tanya screamed. Seconds later, Tanya yelled to the top of her lungs, "Yes, Hell Yeah!" As her left leg shook like an over packed washing machine. About a minute later, it was my turn again. I pulled my dick out of Tanya and started to jerk it as I came, but Tanya wasn't having that. She flipped over like a gymnast, diving her mouth onto my dick, like it was a life or death situation if she didn't swallow those babies.

I kneeled there in the middle of my bed, while Tanya sucked on my dick for about two or three more minutes, crippling me. I had to stop her because I hate being disabled. I love it under those circumstances but I overall hated it because of my dominance.

I then crawled under the sheets pulling Tanya with me to cuddle. After laying there with Tanya for the next ten minutes, I remembered that I had forgotten about Rambo.

"SHIT!" I yelled.

Tanya created some space and looked at me with a puzzled look on her face. I then cracked a smile to ease her thought, as I pulled her back close to me and mumbled in a calm voice, "I forgot all about Rambo. Fuck it now. I'll call him in the AM or some'n."

I then kissed Tanya on her forehead as we shared our love for one another. Seconds later, we were both fading asleep.

CHAPTER 6

It was Saturday night and I was ready to get it in or should I say,

"TURN UP!"

I slept and relaxed around the house all day to get my thoughts together as well as prepare my body for a hell-of-a night. I took a nap around three and woke up about 7:30ish PM and ate dinner. Tanya had cooked before I took a shit, shaved and showered.

I was on my way out the door a little while afterwards. Tanya decided to stay home with Little Bo, since we already had ourselves a great celebration the other night anyway. Besides, she doesn't deal with my friends so why bother. A lot of people don't know that Ms. Miller from PG Detention Center is my woman, and that's how I plan to keep it. Only my two good men, Conrad and Kalvin, know Tanya and that's because they don't deal with the street life or by any means go to prison. They are both tax paying, married men with great careers.

Conrad works as a caregiver to the elderly and handicap. His life consists of work, kids, sports and drinking at the bar. Kalvin, on the other hand, is a photographer. He runs a photography company called Phlavor Photography as well as a magazine company called Golden Honey Magazine. Kalvin is also a Muslim who is always on his deen.

What I respect is that it didn't take prison for him to find Allah. But what I respect most about the two of them is that they were both raised in the same environment that I was, but they didn't become a product of their environment. We all have been tight since I was young and even though my path was different, they respected that and stayed tight. They're the only two that also know where I live.

In 15 minutes flat, I'm around my hood. After once circling the block, I pulled into the third parking lot in Mayfair. While cruising through the parking lot, I saw a dark blue 320 Mercedes Benz that I didn't recognize parked by the trash dumpster, flicking it's headlights as if they were trying to get my attention. I then parked rear end in first next to the Benz. While backing into the parking space, I opened the middle console that separates the driver and passenger seats to pull out my chrome snub nose .357 Magnum, just in case somebody was on some bullshit.

With the 320 Benz parked to my left, the passenger side window rolled down at the same time I was rolling down my driver side window. I slightly leaned my body to my right in the direction of my passenger seat, preparing and positioning myself for action, just to see another two good men of mine, Ghost and OG Face. Ghost was in the passenger seat with a cup of Patron in his hand while OG Face was in the driver seat with a cup in his hand also.

"I see you brought out the space shuttle tonight," Ghost said with a smile on his face as he eyed my CLS63 from front to back. "That muthafucka looking highly beautiful tonight, I must say."

"Well thank you, my lad." I said in the character of a British accent.

"Happy Birthday big guy." OG Face shouted from the driver side in a joking manner.

"Appreciation, pimpin'." I replied with a smile.

"Here you go," Ghost said, reaching his arm towards me and handing me a large brown paper bag. "You might as well start early, we got our own bottle over here so do you, slim!"

I grabbed the bag and opened it to see an unopened bottle of Patron Tequila inside. "That's a bet bruh, I appreciate it." I said as I pulled the bottle out of the bag and removed the cork to open it.

I immediately started sipping straight from the bottle while we sat in our cars inside of the parking lot, reminiscing about old times until about a quarter to eleven.

By then, I was twisted like a hurricane and the entire parking lot was now turned up. Everybody and their mother was in the parking lot. Drinks, bottles, loud pack, e-pills and Marley was everywhere. Everybody that drove or walked to the parking lot made their way over to my car to show me some love and give me their birthday wishes. At 11' o clock on the nose, I pressed the "START" button in my Benz. As soon as my car engine started, somebody yelled through the parking lot, "What's up, Lou! You ready now bruh?"

"Yea buddy!" I shouted out of the car window, which made everybody in the parking lot scramble to their cars or whatever car they planned to ride in to the club. I pulled out of my parking space and drove to the top of the parking lot exit and stopped before leaving out. When I looked into my rearview mirror, I saw about eight or nine vehicles lined up behind mine like a bumble bee line. I then sped out of the parking lot and down the highway to the club. I pulled up in front of Lux Lounge on New York Avenue in Northwest at 11:14PM. After everybody parked, we all met at the front entrance. Me, OG Face, and a couple of other people used valet parking. It was well over 20 people partying with us tonight.

I was glad that we reserved three VIP tables because the club was already packed to the max with another 100 people waiting outside in line. WPGC 95.5 was live on the radio tonight along with rappers Top Dolla Sweizy, O'Don, and Lola Monroe appearing in the club tonight. Two partners of mine, Nate and Fat Bubba, met me at the club as well.

I saw a lot of familiar faces that I hadn't seen in a while. Some of the city's finest women showed face, as well as my big cousin Vell. He had his right hand man Cateye KK bring him out tonight being he was too wasted to walk let alone drive. He didn't keep it a secret either; Vell was spilling drinks on everybody all night. We were all having a good time though, and this was one night I didn't want to end. They usually shut the club down at 2:30 in the morning so at 2:00, I immediately made my way toward the exit to avoid the stampede. While I was moving through the crowd, Vell stopped me and asked me to drop him off at his house. He said that he couldn't find Tony Barber and would rather be safe than sorry. I had no problem with making sure my big cousin made it home safely, even though I myself was white boy wasted.

The club was literally around the corner from my house but was still in reasonable driving distance from Vell's house. Vell's residence was about ten minutes down the street on the Northeast side off of New York Avenue. Vell stayed on Montana Avenue to be exact.

When we pulled up to Vell's house, I had to piss bad as hell so I walked in with him. On the way to the door, my arm was snagged on a piece of wire poking out on his front gate. "You need to get that fixed, cuzo." I said to Vell while looking at my arm.

"I thought about it." Vell replied before taking a brief pause to stop and look at my arm. He then continued, "Then again, it's another weapon. You see it sliced you, right?" He pointed out the scar on my right arm.

"Got damn, cuzo! I know you got some alcohol or peroxide in here somewhere?" I questioned.

"Yea, I got you. It's in the bathroom cabinet upstairs." Vell said as he simultaneously walked into his home pointing up his stairway.

With no response, I quickly ran up the steps, skipping stairs like I was being chased. As soon as I got in the bathroom, I immediately drained my weasel. After washing my hands, I retrieved the peroxide out of the medicine cabinet and thoroughly cleaned my wound.

Afterwards, I walked back downstairs, not so much in the rush that I went up them, holding my arm and applying pressure to the bleeding with toilet tissue.

"I had some band aids up there too cuzo." Vell said as he flopped down onto his living room couch.

"I'm cool, I'll clean it some more when I get in the house." I said as I started walking toward the front door.

"Aye, Lou!" Vell yelled in a tone that made me concerned as to what he had to say.

I stopped in my tracks and turned back in the direction of Vell, giving him my full undivided attention. "What's your plan when it's all over?" Vell asked me with a concerned look on his face, catching me unprepared for his question.

"Plans?" I asked, before taking a three second pause to dissect what Vell asked and then I replied, "You know what cuzo, I don't have any plan at the time. Momma always told me, 'God laughs at our plans', so I'm just living my life as it comes, feel me?"

Vell slowly shook his head up and down then responded, "I can dig that. See, in a way that's so true, but check this out. Not to contest Aunt Mar or anything, but you ever heard of, 'If you fail to plan, you plan to fail'?"

"I can dig that." I replied, as I sobered up a little, sponging up the knowledge Vell was spitting before he continued,

"See, you need to get yourself a plan together because nothing in this world lasts forever and when the walls come crashing down, at least you'll have a carpenter to build it back up, ya dig me? There's nothing wrong with insurance. That brings security and comfort. Plus, you got Little Bo to think about. I want you to think about that."

"For sure." I replied as I reached over to Vell to dap him up, expressing my love and respect for him. After saying our goodbyes I then left his house, got into my Benz and began my pursuit to my house.

While analyzing and taking heed to our conversation, I decided to stop at the BP gas station on New York Avenue to gas up the whip and grab myself a bottle of water. All of a sudden, I felt dehydrated from all of the alcohol my body had consumed. I walked up to the counter and asked for a bottle of water, gave the gas station cashier a 20 dollar bill in which he handed me a bottle of Deer Park water and I requested that the rest be placed towards pump 2, where I was parked. While walking back to my car drinking my water, I saw two men dressed in black hoodie attire walking in my direction.

Dismissing the thought of pumping my gas, I immediately sat inside my Benz, opened the middle console and pulled out my .357 revolver, placing it in my lap with my finger clutching the trigger. One of the guys walked up on my car as I rolled down my window.

"Aye man, you got a cigarette?"

He didn't appear a threat so I didn't shoot. He got close enough to see the revolver sitting on my lap which made him suddenly back up. "That's okay big dawg, I'm aight," the man said nervously as he and his partner swiftly walked back around the corner they came from. I then got out of my car and placed that gas pump nozzle inside the gas tank, locking the handle of the nozzle so that it could automatically pump the gas before getting back inside of the car, impatiently waiting for the pump to stop. No more than two minutes later, an all-black, tinted out Ford Explorer and a few marked police cars all sped inside of the gas station, boxing in my car.

"Get out of the vehicle slowly, and keep your hands high where I can see them!" The police yelled, as they rose out of their vehicles, guns drawn towards me. These bastards were every goddamn where with guns all in my face. I immediately dropped the .357 from my lap onto the floor by the gas pedal, trying to avoid any misunderstandings that could get me shot. I slowly climbed out of my Benz, hands high, before slowly laying on the ground by the front of my car face down as instructed. By this time I was sober as hell. I could probably pass a sobriety test right now as sober as I felt.

"Got it!" is what I heard one of the cops yell as I was getting cuffed with a knee in my back as if I was running somewhere. When they sat me in the back of the police car, I could see them snapping pictures of my revolver as it laid on the floor of my Benz. It was definitely my time to lay it down and there was nothing that Stephen Cooper, or my Benjamin Franklins, could do about this one except get me a good goddamn plea bargain.

CHAPTER 7

Look at my dumb ass sitting in the bullpen cage looking dumber than Kelly Bundy. I should be laid up with Tanya but instead I'm sitting underground in a court building waiting for somebody to instruct me on what I can and can't do. After being bounced around from cell to cell with these cuffs on my ankles, I was finally working my way closer to seeing a judge. The US Marshals shackled my handcuffs to a chain, which was wrapped around my waist, and moved me to a holding cell behind the judge's chamber. "Bigsby!" A US Marshal yelled from outside of the holding cell as he used his key to open the cage door. I rose to my feet and two stepped my way out of the holding cell into the court room. There were a lot of people sitting in the court room looking at me as I walked in from through a large wooden door on the side of the judge's clerk station. "Step in that box right there." A US Marshal ordered, as I stood with my back toward the court room of spectators facing Judge House.

After Judge House read off my accused charges, my stand-in attorney argued why I should be released and how pre-trial accepted me to be released under their supervision agency, being that in DC we don't have bail bondsmen and you rarely ever get cash bonds. Pre-trial is your bond, and the nature of your charge, criminal background, escape history, occupation and several other things determine whether or not you are eligible for their program. Even if accepted, the judge still has the last say-so of whether to hold or release you to their supervision.

If accepted, you can get a bail for either halfway house, home monitor program or personal release with an in court sworn promise to appear in court on the date listed, as well as abide by all pre-trial supervision guidelines. Regardless of what your bail status is, you would still have to report to see a supervision officer as well as take a urine analysis at least once a week unless instructed otherwise.

The prosecution argues how I had a prior gun conviction in PG County, Maryland and how I had a .357 Magnum to protect the drugs that were in my trunk.

"WHAT!" I accidentally yelled out in the courtroom, surprised at what I heard.

"Your Honor, there was, what is assumed to be, one pound of high grade marijuana inside of a black duffel bag, which is currently being tested at a laboratory of the DC Metropolitan Police Department to confirm the substance. We believe Mr. Bigsby had the .357 revolver to protect the delivery and distribution of the marijuana substance." The prosecution argued before continuing, "Your Honor, we are asking that you will place a hold on Mr. Bigsby at least until the MPD comes back with its test results to confirm these allegations. We also strongly believe that Mr. Bigsby is a flight risk. He was arrested at a gas station on New York Avenue in Northeast, DC in a black 2012 CLS63 model Mercedes-Benz, which is registered to the name of LaTanya Chanel Miller of 901 New Jersey Avenue in the Northwest section of DC, zip code 20001. Your honor that is the same exact address that we have recorded for Mr. Bigsby," the prosecution said before taking a slight pause to collect her thoughts and then continued, "We strongly believe that Mr. Bigsby has the financial stability to jump bail and disappear past the duration of this case statute of limitations. Mr. Bigsby is unemployed and never has been employed, with nine years of school completed."

BAM! There goes the dagger. After seeing Judge House cut her eyes at me, giving me a deep stare of disappointment and shame, I knew I wasn't getting released after that. Judge House was writing something on a piece of paper during the 30 second moment of silence inside of the courtroom. Without even looking up, the judge grabbed her gavel and declared, "Bail denied, five days hold." Before slamming it to the hollow piece of wood beneath it.

The US Marshal then immediately escorted me through the tall wooden door on the opposite side of the judge's bench from which I had entered. While walking through the doorway, I could hear the clerk saying, "Probable Cause Hearing date set for calendar date Monday, September 22, 2014.

The state versus..." Here I laid around in DC jail's processing unit all damn day Sunday, after being transported from the police station where I was laying on steel benches for eight hours just to be denied release on Monday. Sheesh! I can't win for losing and Mr. Cooper probably doesn't know I'm locked up yet. I doubt if Tanya knows. It's not like I come to jail often, even though for the past few years I've been getting caught up with these damn guns. I need to make a call ASAP as soon as I get to the housing unit. I need to see Steve at my Preliminary Hearing, pronto. I'm trying to get my yellow ass out of prison. As soon as I got into my cell I made my bed and fell straight to sleep. I was tired and exhausted from all of that cell hopping. No celly for me was a blessing for him because I was damn sure going to be calling the hogs tonight.

The next morning before lunch chow, it was like God heard my prayers. "Bigsby!" I heard the bald correctional officer yell from in front of his station.

"Yea, what's up?" I yelled back, excited to hear my name called.

"Legal visit, suit up!" the correctional officer replied. I immediately ran from the one rim basketball court to my cell to put on my orange jumpsuit. Afterwards, I went to retrieve the blue hall pass from the correctional officer with a check beside the words VISITING HALL. I then left the unit and speed walked down the hallway to the visiting room. The visiting hall is for legal visits only. All social visits are on a TV monitor with a phone receiver connected to it, located in the middle of each housing unit.

When I arrived to the visiting hall, another bald head correctional officer was standing outside of the hall and retrieved the slip from my hand before signing it. As I walked into the visiting hall I saw my attorney Steve sitting alone inside one of the isolated meeting rooms. I walked in, shook his hand and took a seat as he got straight to the point. "You know you fucked up, right?" Steve said in a smooth and calm manner, like the detective addressed Kane on Menace II Society.

"Yeah I know Steve, that's my bad champ. What do you think you can do for me though?" I pled.

"I mean, shit! I can fight it, probably beat it, but chances are we wouldn't even get that far without District Court picking up the case. The government would dismiss it before trial to avoid acquittal if they feel they can't beat us." Steve said with a worried and concerned look on his face.

"Then we would probably end up taking a plea in District Court anyway, due to their high conviction rate, sharp prosecutors and railroad strategies." I said, complimenting Steve's theory.

"Well, I couldn't have said that any better. They are a tough cookie, Lou. I can't guarantee you anything, but I can save you some cash and try to work out a plea bargain so the feds don't pick up your case. I'm going to do my job and argue for the bottom of the guidelines and I should be able to talk to the prosecution to see if we can come to some agreement but like I said at first, I can't promise you anything." Steve said.

"Well I'ma trust your decision and let you work out a plea bargain." I said after taking a deep breath of frustration.

"But first we have to see everything they have on you at the preliminary hearing next Monday," Steve said with energy, trying to ignite some hope into me. "Oh yeah, there's still one more problem."

"What's that, Steve?" I asked with a concerned look on my face.

"Monday for your preliminary hearing, you're in front of Judge Knowles. She's not that bad, but the problem comes in when we talk about your sentencing judge. You're in front of Dixon." He said to me with a disappointing look on his face letting me know everything.

"And?" I asked arrogantly as if I didn't care.

"And! He's an asshole. I mean West Coast Productions, Cherokee and Lethal Lips, real live porn star type of assholes." Steve said, making me laugh a little, loosening the tension in the atmosphere.

"Yeah, I heard about slim but fuck him! It's just a pistol and weed case, it ain't like I'm fighting a body or some'n." I said.

"Alrighty then, see you on Monday, Lou." Steve said before we rose to our feet and shook hands. After getting strip searched by the C.O., I strolled back to my housing unit, went straight in my cell and laid back on my bunk thinking. Steve must really like me or my money because he don't ever have any free time to come and see anyone, unless preparing for trial and he's always in trial. Usually he'll send one of his investigators to come and represent him. I was pretty surprised to see him. It was probably because he knows for sure that I'm a drug dealer, and will help his ass stay rich. It doesn't matter to me, as long as I'm a free man. I'm cool with that. I don't plan on staying around in this game too much longer anyway, especially not slipping like I just did.

I mean, I just can't believe I was so damn careless and forgot about that pound in the trunk. I was big shoe tripping. I was supposed to been got rid of that a long time ago. I'm pretty disappointed in myself because I don't usually slip up like that. I guess that came from dealing with so much weight, I overlooked it as a small thing to a giant. Or maybe it was from all of the celebrating I was doing for my birthday. That was also my first time ever having drugs in the Benz. Whatever the reason was, I knew for sure it was time to pave my exit away from this business.

I was really contemplating on what Vell had preached to me a few nights ago: "If you fail to plan, you plan to fail." That was true indeed. It was now my time to make a plan, because I hated failure and didn't plan to appreciate it.

CHAPTER 8

"Bigsby! Pack it up!" A sexy, short haired female C.O. yelled up to my cell as my cell door automatically opened. I stood up out of my bed, stuck my head out of the door and yelled back,

"Where I'm going!?"

"Northwest-one and hurry up Mr. Bigsby!" she yelled back from in front of their control booth station. I instantly grabbed my hygiene pack, bed robe, sheets and towels before rushing out of there.

I was eager as hell to get in General Population. I needed to use the phone bad as hell. As soon as I got to NW1, I was assigned to cell 53 top bunk. While walking down the tier to my cell, the C.O.'s opened the door from their control booth, making my cellmate stick his head out of the cell to see what was going on.

To my surprise, it was light skinned Domo, one of Mayfair's good men. That was my roll dog. When he saw me he smiled in shock to see me walking to his cell and he stepped out to greet me with a hand smack and hug. Domo and I grew up together in Cruddy Island. We went to the same elementary school, middle school and probably dropped out of high school at the same time for the love of money.

I remember driving past his building in Mayfair and seeing the undercover cops walking him and his mother out of his building in handcuffs after they raided his apartment. He and I have the same charge except he had crack and I had marijuana. We chopped it up and talked all day about everything under the sun. We were both excited to see someone from around our hood, that we grew up with and was raised with, only if the circumstances could have been better.

After I finally made my bed, I went to turn my phone list in to our

Unit Case Manager before she left. Three days later, my phone

numbers were registered into their system and cleared for use, so I got

me a slot in a phone line. In DC jail, you have to find yourself a slot

in a phone line on one of the eight payphones on each unit. Most of

the phones in the jail are ran by a certain group of people such as

religious organizations or whichever side of the city you are from. If

you don't fit in any of the categories, then you better be a well-known

official dude or you better not touch their phones without their

permission. That's how it is and always was to my knowledge. I

talked with Tanya and Little Bo a lot throughout the week and before

I knew it, it was Monday, and I was back in court.

"...Inside of the trunk we retrieved a black, nylon material, military styled Tactical 550 duffel bag, which housed a marijuana looking substance inside of it. We then transferred the substance back to our laboratory and tested it. The results came back positive as a high grade of marijuana, with the weight of four hundred and forty eight grams, which has an estimated street value of eight thousand, nine hundred and sixty US dollars." The MPD detective testified at my preliminary probable cause hearing. He also verified that he got a tip from a confidential informant about a man in a Mercedes Benz at the BP gas station on New York Avenue, brandishing a silver handgun.

 This shit was getting out of hand. All of the people that look thuggish was cops, and all of the supposed to be gangsters were now displaying the gay and nerdy looks. This shit was definitely confusing me. I then knew it was about time to call it quits.

After another denied bail, the judge then set me a hearing date for next month, and Steve said that someone would come up to the jail and talk with me tomorrow as he quickly sped out of the courtroom, chasing the money train in the next one. I was then escorted out of the courtroom and downstairs by a US Marshal to another bullpen holding cell.

I was really starting to feel like a gorilla every time I came here. A couple of hours later, I was transported back to DC jail. As soon as I returned, I explained to Domo what had just happened in court, before reserving myself a slot on the end phone by the stairwell. I then called Tanya, to inform her on what was happening and she instantly began to cry. While calming her down, I happened to lift my head up and saw some light skinned, red headed opey looking dude with a low haircut staring in my face while leaning on a railing beside the end phone I was on.

I took an inventory glance at my surroundings and at him and then looked away, not thinking anything major of the situation as I continued on with my conversation. As soon as I finished my 15 minute telephone call, I then stood up, slowly paced away from the phone and noticed main man was grilling me harder than a burnt burger at a cook-out.

"What's up, slim, you know me from somewhere?" I snapped in a mellow but dominant and irritated tone.

"Naw," he replied before pausing and frowning his face then continued, "That's why I'm looking at you, champ.

I don't know you. Where you from?" he asked me aggressively.

"Don't worry 'bout where I'm from slim. What it's a problem or something?"

"Yea it is, if you ain't from Southeast."

"Naw I ain't, I'm from Northeast! What you want some work or something?" I combatively offered as I nodded my head towards the cells letting him know that I didn't mind sliding inside of a cell to fight.

I then took a step closer towards him as he stood up away from the railing and said, "Hold up!" as he turned away from me and walked up the stairway to the TV room and tapped some tall dark skinned dude with dreadlocks on his shoulder and said something in his ear. The tall guy then turned around to look behind himself towards me with an angry looking mean mug on his face, which instantly turned into a smile.

"Nigga! Get the fuck away from me before I smack that face, you stupid nigga!" The tall guy angrily said to the red headed boy as he proceeded to walk down the stairway towards me.

"My nigga, Lou! What's up, bruh?" It was the one and only Sykey Mikey from Parkchester.

"What's up, Syke! What's up with your wild ass man?" I said to Mikey, as I reached out to give him a firm grip five.

"I don't know what's up with slim. He green. You gotta give a nigga like him a pass, he don't know no better," Mikey said, with a slight grin on his face then continued, "He keep telling people he from The Nut. I had to press his bitch ass out when I first hit the unit. The nigga an alien. I got this UFO nigga paying me taxes for claiming my hood. Fuck 'em though." Mikey said as we laughed.

"See niggas like him be getting niggas life. The ol' fuck boy, Brandy, I just wanna be down ass niggas," I said before pausing as we laughed then continued, "See a nigga like him, you gotta knock his shit loose first chance you get 'cause when the feds come down on you, he gonna be first in line to sign-up."

"And that's no bullshit," Mikey said confirming my statement. Sykey Mikey and I stood there and talked until count time.

He let me know that he and the big homie from my hood, Jmo, were cellies back in 2012, before Jmo went to the feds, and how he and Barbershop Drew from around my way were on SW1 together before Drew left and went to the feds. He also let me know about how a young nigga named Donnie, who used to be around my hood, dropped a note to the C.O.'s snitching on my partner Rambo, a couple of years ago. He said that Donnie was on some paranoid and scared shit, thinking Rambo was going to do something to him, so he dropped a note telling the officers that Rambo had a knife and got him sent to the hole. I told him I wasn't surprised at all. Donnie ain't built for this life no matter how much he tries to fake it. Mikey and I shared a good amount of laughs before locking in our cells. Mikey was a good associate of mine on the streets. He used to purchase pounds of loud from me, no less than three at a time before being arrested.

After having the minor experience with the red headed guy, who I later found out was named Killa Reds, I purchased me a little protection. A bone crusher! A bone crusher is a giant screw, sharpened into the form of a knife. Everybody wears orange jumpsuits in DC jail except for the Sexual Misconduct Unit (SMU). They wear red jumpsuits and almost everyone has a slit on the side of their jumpsuits like a pocket for one of two reasons, if not both; either, it's used for easy access if you're toting a knife or you're in the game. The game, as far as jerking your penis on the female C.O.'s. That's a common thing in DC jail but that's one game I'm not in. After I purchased the bone crusher, it was almost as if Killa Reds knew it, because he was acting highly nervous and scared around me. He was also spending a lot of quality time around the C.O.'s control station. They say pressure busts pipes and on this particular day, I was angry and having a bad day. The pressure and tension I was giving out made Killa Reds pull out his pipe and jerk off directly in front of the C.O.'s control station.

The female C.O. hit a button on her walkie-talkie and called a panic code that had the goon squad rush into our housing unit, pepper spray Killa Reds and drag him out of the unit like a pissy mattress. Killa Reds pulled what we like to call a five star check-in move. One of the greatest I've ever seen.

After about four months of going back and forth to court from NW1, I finally pled guilty to Possession of Marijuana with the intent to distribute while armed. Approximately two months later, I was being sentenced to 36 months in prison with six months' time credit and counting. Judge Dixon held up to his asshole image. In my six months in DC jail I saw at least 15 people get terribly stabbed, and only one stabbing was fatal. About ten of the stabbings including the fatal one was due to an altercation over the phone, and the rest were either over the television or personal street beef. On a Friday morning, ten days after my sentencing, I was on my way to the feds to finish up my time. An experience that I was bound to see, and Lord knows I needed.

CHAPTER 9

"Where I'm headed to, C.O.?" I asked the white female officer who was logging my personal information into her computer at Northern Neck Regional Jail, also known as Warsaw in Virginia. It's also a federal holdover spot and a detention center for high profile cases that held people such as Michael Vick and Chris Brown.

"FCI Cumberland," the overweight officer responded, as she pointed her finger towards the wall in front of her desk and said, "stand over there behind the white line so that I can snap your picture."

After the processing procedure and changing out of the paper flight suits that the US Marshals issue for travel purposes into Warsaw, blue prison jumper, me and three other men who also came from DC jail were issued a bed robe before being escorted to our assigned units. I stayed in Warsaw for the weekend before being transferred to Cumberland, Maryland on Monday morning. I'm glad I wasn't there for too much longer—even though the food was cooked perfectly the portion amount was smaller than a Lunchable. I couldn't have given that to Little Bo. I probably would have heard him say his first five letter curse word. These people were tough. One of the three men from DC jail went to FCI Cumberland with me while the other two went to Petersburg Low in Virginia, and FCI Butner in North Carolina. There were a few other people on the bus with us when we exchanged at Harrisburg Airport in Harrisburg, Pennsylvania, but none of them were from DC. The one guy that was travelling with me since DC jail introduced himself as JV. JV was a cool dude. He loved to joke around a lot and make people laugh. While talking to him on our bus ride, I also learned that he had a serious gambling habit. JV told me that he was from 22nd Street in Southeast. He also let me know, after learning where I'm from, that he associates with two partners of mine from Cruddy Island named AK and Ruga Rell. I let him know that the two of them were like brothers to me. JV and I conversed and connected real heavy becoming really tight. He gave the impression of a real good loyal dude, which later made me befriend him.

We arrived at FCI Cumberland around 5:30 that afternoon. After the processing procedure, medical evaluations, clothing and bed robe exchange, we were then assigned to our housing units around 8:30PM. JV was assigned to housing unit A-2, while I was sent to housing unit B-2, room 211 the upper bunk. When I walked into the unit I felt like 2Pac, "All Eyes On Me!" and to top it off, there was this big ass dude about 6' 2" 250 pounds solid performing exercises under the stairwell, rapping 2Pac. "Revenge is like the sweetest joy next to getting pussy!" The big guy said before he did each set of ten.

The short white male C.O., who first greeted me at the door, glanced at my ID card before pointing upstairs to a cell in the corner of the top tier. While walking on the bottom tier towards the staircase, I was greeted by a fat guy with curly hair, "What's up playa, where you from?"

"I'm from DC." I responded.

"Well your homies are upstairs in the TV room over there." He said

as he pointed to an enclosed room on the top tier in the exact

opposite direction of my assigned room.

"Okay cool, thanks moe." I said. I then proceeded to walk up the flight of stairs to my room. When I got to my bedroom, there were two older men in the room that looked as if they were in their early fifties. The first one to introduce himself was about 5'5" tall with salt & pepper dreadlocks and had a squeaky voice that reminded me of the comedian Katt Williams. He said his name was Quinn and he had been in for 25 years. Quinn was from California and had been all around the federal system. The other guy was about 6 feet tall and he too had a salt & pepper bush of hair. He kept it neat like a throwback Steve Harvey without the crispy shape up. He introduced himself as Rudy from Southwest, DC. Rudy had been incarcerated for 20 years and was waiting to see the Parole Commission. I then introduced myself as Lou and explained why I was incarcerated and about how much time I had to do. After about five minutes of minor conversation, Rudy and Quinn then excused themselves out of the room, giving me space to make my bed, use the toilet and establish myself. That showed a sign of respect, which is a common trait in the feds, especially to men who've done time inside of a maximum security prison. I was placed into a three man room which consisted of one two man bunk and one single bed that sat beside the bunk. I was assigned to the top bunk which was over top of Rudy.

After about two minutes in the room alone establishing myself, I heard a knock on my room door. As I turned around to look towards the door it was already opening. I then saw Baby D, Rodney and Tony! Damn! I ain't seen these three dudes since God knows when. Baby D was from Wingate Towers and Galveston Street area in Southwest but also used to hang out in the Lincoln Heights neighborhood of Northeast.

I knew him since we were young because that's where Vell and D-Bo once stomped ground at. And my grandmother lived there for 33 years before she died. Rodney is from Martin Luther King Jr Avenue in Southeast. His father and sisters lived around my hood since forever. We knew each other since we were young as well. His brother was in my class in elementary school. Tony was from Simple City. Tony is my partners Domo and Lil Mark's cousin. He once lived around my neighborhood with this girl named Quil before being arrested in 2004. After standing in my room talking to the three of them for about an hour, I heard the C.O. yell, "five minutes!" We then shook hands as they departed to prepare themselves for lockdown. In FCI Cumberland, they lockdown at about 9:50pm to prepare you for the 10 o'clock stand-up count. After the C.O. locked us in our cells and secured the door, Rudy and Quinn explained to me how there are a lot of people in the feds, especially FCI's and low security facilities, waiting to go home off the next man.

The explained how the majority of the compound were rats in some type of way. "If not paperwork hot, they're institution hot," Rudy said. "Don't let these clowns go home off of you, Lou, because they are coming to court," Quinn said, while raising his right hand, imitating someone sitting on a stand ready to testify after getting sworn in. Rudy explained how there are over 300 DC inmates on Cumberland's compound and about the same amount of Baltimore inmates who have always been our allies.

I explained to them how that was good to know but that I was on my own time while here. I only deal with real men so that's how I planned to keep it. We talked for about an hour after the stand-up count before falling asleep. In the feds, there are two stand-up counts from Monday through Friday. There are three stand-up counts on Saturdays, Sundays and holidays. One thing I learned about prison is that the officers will play a lot of games; they'll play you for your visits and if in the right location you could get lucky enough to get your penis played with but what they don't play with is their count. Interfere with their count and your ass is grass and you'll get your ass buried!

The next morning I awoke around 6AM. After brushing my teeth, washing my face and taking a piss, I heard the shift C.O. yell, "CHOW!" I walked out of my cell to see people running out of the front door as if they were serving release paper smothered in pussy. I went to the cafeteria, ate and then came back to the unit. Baby D then let me know that I have to go to the laundry department at the 7:30AM work call move to get my khaki clothing, tee shirt and underclothes. Before the move was announced, Rodney handed me a pair of old beat down Nike's. I slid them on my feet ASAP! It was either them or the Bruce Lee karate slippers that were starting to hurt my feet.

When I got to laundry, they issued me a pair of black steel toe boots. At the 8:30 move, I rushed back to the unit to try to drop off my clothes and go to recreation. A "move" is an announcement made on the compound loud speaker which instructs inmates to move around throughout the compound. At FCI Cumberland, the move was for ten minutes. They announce the move once every hour.

When they say, "RECALL", that means to go where you belong, which in most cases means your housing unit. "WORK CALL" means to go to your job, or you can go to any other available place on the compound if it's opened. If you're caught somewhere that you don't belong, you can be placed in the Special Housing Unit (SHU), also known as the hole. At 9:30am, another move was called, and I walked to the recreation.

When I got to recreation, I sat on a bench which was seated in front of a set of pull-up and dip bars that were on the immediate outside of the basketball gym. Outside, I saw two, full basketball courts and a softball field that was encompassed by a large running track. There was also a soccer field with another track circled around it and a handball area with about four walls for handball. When I walked into the basketball gym, I looked around and was surprised at the quality and size of the gym. It was state of the art for it to be inside of a prison.

After a few minutes of checking out the gym, I walked back outside

past the pull-up bars and heard, "Revenge is like the sweetest joy next

to getting pussy," being recited from behind me. I turned to look over

my right shoulder and saw the big black guy that I saw last night in my

unit doing pull-ups. I laughed and thought to myself, "This nigga

burnt out." I walked back toward the bench that I was previously

sitting on and saw the clown of the century walking towards me with a

huge smile on his face, extending his hand for a shake.

"Wassup, homie? I see you made it to the feds my nigga." Killa

Reds said excitedly, as if he and I were the best of friends. I then

looked at that fool and his hand as if they were a deadly disease.

"What you mean Homie? Holmes! You ain't my nigga! We ain't

cool!" I spat aggressively at Killa Reds, turning that fake ass smile into

a grin.

"What you mean, bruh?" Killa Reds said.

"Nigga please, we ain't there slim! You and I never been cool!"

"Damn slim, this da feds, bruh," he pleaded.

"The feds? Nigga, I don't see that shit! I'm a muthafuckin' man champ! I ain't with that beef everywhere except the feds shit! Miss me with that one!" I said as I pointed my fingers in his face and made him take a step backward in defense to my aggressive actions.

"Kill moe, that's crazy." Killa Reds said, shaking his head from left to right as if he couldn't believe what was happening. A mugshot looking frown then appeared on his face as he gave me a two second long deep stare. If looks could kill, it would have been a closed casket for me.

"I'm saying, like I told you once before, we can work like it ain't nothing!" I spat at Killa Reds. At this point, everyone that was in our area had stopped what they were doing to look at the commotion that was being riled up.

"You got it slim, be easy." Killa Reds said, as he walked away from me towards the softball field and large track. Something told me that Killa Reds ain't take that lightly but I didn't give a damn. If he wanted to go to war, I was ready. Sleep is for dreamers and I ain't have no dreams or aspirations at the time so sleeping is something I just don't do. I was alert and ready for whatever, whenever. I'm a man, first. That's how it's always been and always will be until I die.

CHAPTER 10

The next morning I had Baby D call Tanya to let her know to go to Western Union and fill up my account. Tanya then placed $1000 on my books. A month later another $320, which was the money from my DC jail account, had popped up in my account. My case manager gave me a copy of my computation sheet as well as my PAC number. PAC is your phone access code which is used for accessing not just your telephone service but your email service as well. The number sticks with you for the rest of your life unless you request a new one. A computation sheet is a form that shows the charges you've been convicted of as well as the length of sentence you were issued for each charge. It also displays your full time release date, your satisfactory release date which includes the 15% of good time and your home detention eligibility date, which in other words is your halfway house date. I was scheduled to go to the halfway house of January 6, 2017.

I was awarded three months of halfway house from my satisfactory release date which was April 6, 2017. After recording my voice on the telephone service and uploading some of my contacts into the computer system, I immediately called A.K. and Ruga Rell to do my homework on J.V. They both stamped his approval and let me know that someone salted his name down. They let me know that he was a good man who was helping another good man get acquitted on his case. I then called Tanya and talked to her for a little while. After I got off of the phone with her, I made a mental note to check up on J.V's paperwork myself even though their word is gold. But it's nothing like saying, "I saw his work" yourself, just in case this matter came back to light. I then called Tanya two more times that morning, and she updated me on everything from my mom, to Little Bo, to the bills, and how her hormones were jumping from talking to me on the phone.

The last conversation that Tanya and I had was at D.C. Jail. After

that conversation I had to immediately take a shower upon ending our

call. It seems as if this would be the case once again. Yesterday I met

a lot of cool dudes in my unit who introduced themselves in the TV

room. It was uptown blood, Elmo, from Wellington Park, MLK

Lurch, Simple City Fred, an old timer named Earl from 1-5

Millionaires, D.C., Darius and Quay, all from Congress Park, and Jay

from Potomac Gardens.

Tu-Tu from Trinidad, Chestnut from Baltimore, Anacostia Marco,

another old timer named Top Cat, Phil who they were calling Bay-

Bay, Vaughn from Parkland, Uncle Wimp, Landover Reds and

Quick from God knows where. These were a group of people who I

immediately took a liking to. You can tell by the comfort of the

atmosphere that these men got along well.

My cellmates Rudy and Quinn also pointed out a couple of legends in my unit such as Baltimore's own, Peanut King, the street legend and the political prisoner, Sundiata Acoli. They also let me know that one of our neighborhood big homies, Jmo, was here. They said he had to put hands on some young cat from uptown. They said that he was transferred to USP Lee, but was placed in the SHU upon arrival there because the S.I.S. got angry at him for not telling them what had happened in an assault he was allegedly involved in. So they labeled his hands a weapon and gave him diesel therapy. Turned a one month SHU sentence into seven.

After talking to Rudy and Quinn, mainly about how **PRO-RAT** the streets had become, for about another thirty minutes, I then came to a conclusion with myself. From this day forward, I'm going to dedicate myself to paving my exit from the illegal drug trade. I have to find something better before I get bit by one of those rodents. **ASAP!**

CHAPTER 11

A month later, I decided it was time to get healthy as I was now established as far as the MP3 player, sweat suits, fresh shoes, shorts and work out gear. At the 8:30 AM move, I made my way to the recreation to exercise the muscles I'd been looking for. For the past month I had been doing my pull-ups inside my housing unit under the staircase, trying to break myself in before I went outside to the real pull-up and dip bar with the heavy hitters. Hard work and dedication got me up to eight pull-ups at a time. I'd do ten sets of eight, which was good after only one month of working out. I was also doing 25 push-ups at a time. I usually did ten sets of 25 while doing my pull ups. It then became time for me to finally take my talents to South Beach, the rec yard. As soon as I got to the rec yard, I heard the big black guy singing his favorite line, "Revenge is like the sweetest joy next to getting pussy," as I bent the corner to see him pulling up on the pull up bar.

I sat at the table directly in front of the pull up bar he was on, stretching my arms, chest, back and shoulders before placing on my handball gloves. I used the handball gloves for work-out purposes only since I couldn't play a lick of handball. As soon as I placed on my gloves, I lifted my head to see J.V. walking over in my direction with a brown envelope in his hand. When he reached the table, he smiled as we fist bumped before he handed me a folder.

"Here you go." J.V. said as I nodded my head and pulled the documents out of the large brown manila folder. "It ain't too much of nuttin' I gotta prove to these other niggaz, but I fuck wit' you and you be fucking wit' some good men so I felt it was only right that you see who you dealing with. A stand-up nigga."

I proceeded to read everything that he had inside the folder, which included his interview with detectives in which he made a statement removing a guy named Frank from the scene of the crime. To my knowledge, Frank was on trial for murder and was later acquitted, thanks to the help of J.V... To me, he was official and got my stamp of approval. After I finished reading everything, I placed his documents back into the brown folder. We talked for another five minutes or so before J.V. walked off to catch up with Lil Daddy from Southern Avenue, in Southeast.

"You tryna get some action, slim?" The big, black 2Pac rapping man asked after tapping my shoulder with the back of his hand.

"Ain't no question." I responded as I stood up.

"Aight, then you go after Tony Lewis," he said, pointing towards a stocky build man who was leaning with his back onto a bench talking to Peanut King before continuing, "It's just the four of us. Sundiata, Tony, you then me, aight."

"Aight then, that's a bet." I replied.

"My name's Big Mike by the way." He said as he balled his hand into a fist, reaching towards me for a fist bump. I reached out with my fist balled up and gave Big Mike a fist bump before saying,

"I'm Lou."

After Tony Lewis finished doing his clips, I then did my set and we had a consistent flow for about an hour and a half. Before every set, Big Mike sung his anthem, which made me draw a conclusion that that was his motivational song. Old man Sundiata had me embarrassed to touch the bar because for him to be his age, he was doing his sets with ease and great form like a 25 year old man, fresh out of military boot camp. Just the four of us worked out on that bar until recall, which was the 10:30 move. We all gave each other a fist bump before gathering our belongings and proceeding to our housing units. When I got to the recreation door on to the walkway, Big Mike tapped my right shoulder as he walked past me and said, "Good money, slim. Keep it coming, consistency is the key." Before taking off, power walking toward the unit like he was on a marathon. When I got back into the unit, I immediately took a shower and then went to eat lunch at the chow hall.

I kept the same routine Monday through Friday, and on Saturday and Sunday I would relax to rest my muscles. Big Mike and I had never really held a conversation about anything outside of exercising until one day, about two weeks later, I was standing on the top tier by myself looking at a movie titled "Ted" on the institution movie station.

Big Mike walked up beside me and leaned forward with his forearms stationed on the railing. I looked over my right shoulder at Big Mike before taking one of my earbud headphones out of my ear and said, "What's up wit' cha?" as I rotated my right arm towards Big Mike for a fist bump.

"Ain't shit." Big Mike replied as he tapped my fist with his fist then asked, "This joint good?"

"It's aight so far, something to do." I replied.

"True. You been kinda showing results too. Don't get too big around here, the lil' nigga Reds might try you." Big Mike joked as he chuckled.

"Ha!" I responded with laughter. "I'm patiently waiting."

"Shit, he 'bout to roll out in 'bout a month or so, he don't want no smoke."

"Oh yea, he tryna sneak up outta here, huh." I said.

"Some'n like dat." Big Mike replied as he shook his head up and down with a smiling grin before continuing, "Where you from Lil Homie?"

"Over Paradise and Mayfair." I said looking Big Mike in his eyes.

"Oh yea!" he said, sounding excited as his eyes opened wider with a happy look on his face then continued, "So you over Paradise and Mayfield, huh. You over there in the Kenilworth area?"

"Yea, Mayfair." I corrected Big Mike as we laughed.

"Yea, you know what I mean. You over there with Heart, Kenilworth Fats and Chico and 'em?" Big Mike said.

"Yea, I'm over there with them. I don't know Kenilworth Fats but I heard of him though." I said as I took my earbuds completely out of my ears and stood up and away from the railing giving Big Mike my full attention.

"How old are you shawty?"

"I'm twenty-seven."

"So you should be somewhat hipped to all the good men y'all bred around there? Keith Holmes, Tony Blunt, Lil Heidi, Block and one of your homies that just left from down here named Jmo." Big Mike said.

"Yea. Jmo." I replied in confirmation.

"Yea, slim a good nigga. I was fucking with slim before the young nigga got him wrong." Big Mike said as he pointed across the tier for emphasis before continuing, "Aye! You know Lil' Bar?"

"Yea, Bar Banks." I said with a smile.

"Yea Shawty!" Big Mike replied with excitement and laughter before continuing, "Slim was crazy as shit. I heard about him getting killed. I remember one day I was on some joke time shit with Heart. So, I pulled up around the way, leaning low, fake mean muggin' on Heart." Big Mike said, acting out his actions before continuing, "next thing I know, this lil' nigga whipped out this big ass gun and got ta' hitting at my car. I hauled ass!" Big Mike said as we both laughed. "Heart called my cell phone and told me to come back through. I circled around y'all way and then pulled back up. I got out of the car and Heart was laughing me out. He introduced me to shawty though. I had to respect his G. He did what he was suppose to do." Big Mike said as we shared more laughter about the situation with Bar. We had more conversations, mainly about what had been going on in the streets and feeling each other out about who we may know and not know. From the conversations, I learned that Big Mike hung in Northeast before his arrest and that he had been incarcerated for 18 years. We conversed until the C.O. yelled his five minute until lockdown warning. After bumping fists, we both went our separate ways to our cells to prepare ourselves to lock in for the remainder of the night. I had also learned that Big Mike had been from penitentiary to penitentiary on disciplinary transfer, as well as to the

Special Management Unit, also known as the SMU Program. The

SMU Program is a program for troubled and violent inmates. Big

Mike said that Cumberland was his first FCI medium facility and that

he had been here for about three years. He said that he will see the

parole board next year, and since he's been shot free for the past ten

years that he has high expectations on getting released.

A "Shot" is an in-house disciplinary violation report that you get

charged with when you disobey one of the federal institution rules and

regulations. Big Mike expressed that he doesn't deal with too many

people here because of the snitch population in FCI medium

facilities. To me, the feds as a whole has too many stool pigeons. Big

Mike told me to keep my circle as small as a screw top, which is

something that I do anyway. He reminded me of myself in a lot of

ways, which let me know that we'd get along just fine.

CHAPTER 12

Killa Reds finally left and went to the halfway house. He was only serving his probation violation time which was nothing. About another year had passed and I now had under a year left. It's true what they say about fed time—months are like weeks which make years fly like Delta Airlines. After you place yourself into a daily routine and stay active in vocational programs as well as recreational activities, you don't see time anymore.

The only time you do see is the day you come in and the day you're released. The **NFL** football, **NBA** basketball, **MLB** baseball seasons play a major part as well. The feds is like being in Vegas; 85% of inmates gamble either on poker and card tables or bet on sports ticket lines. This here is the feds. You have some of the world's richest criminals from drug dealers to mob bosses to **W**all Street thieves and so on.

How can you possibly stop money from moving? It's impossible, and something the feds already know. As long as the violence is kept to a minimum, "Everybody eats, B!"

Big Mike and I had built a good relationship. It's like we just clicked on every level. He showed me a lot of loyalty so far which is a rare trait. I had shown him my photo album which possessed pictures of my family and friends. I also had pictures of some random females who sent me their pictures with letters that expressed how they would love to hook up with me when I came home. A partner of mine placed my picture and contact information on his Facebook page without permission, just trying to do a good deed. I was getting all types of letters from random women even though I never wrote any of the women back. I was flattered to see that I can still pull women in prison. I was satisfied with Tanya, though. Tanya's intelligent, independent, beautiful and patient. She's every man's dream and every woman's nightmare. She plays her position and she takes care of home. What more can I ask for? While we were looking through my photo album, I saw tears form in Big Mike's eyes. I had family pictures of Tanya, Little Bo, Vell, D-Bo and my aunts and uncles all in one section. While I was explaining who was who, I asked Big Mike if he was okay. That's when he opened up to me, letting me know about his family. He said that after his arrest for this case, his sister and brother were murdered.

Before his arrest, he had just lost his other brother. He also said that his mother had just passed away no more than five years ago and that his wife, Sonya, is the only family that he has on the streets. Big Mike said that he and Sonya had met off of a website called WriteAPrisoner.com. He said that this was eight years ago and that they've been married for three. Sonya is from San Diego, California but moved to Alexandria, Virginia to be closer to Big Mike. He told me how much he loved and appreciated Sonya. He said that she had been holding him down the entire time and hadn't missed a beat.

I grew a new found respect for Big Mike for opening up his emotional thoughts to me. It told a lot about him as a man. Big Mike complimented me on Tanya and my taste in women. He also let me know that he overheard some young dudes in the rec yard talking about how I was the man on the streets and how what I do for a living is right up his alley. He said that he didn't think hustling dope or coke was a wise decision after returning home from a long stretch in prison. I agreed to what he said and to helping him get on his feet and establish himself when he came home. I also let him know that for the past year I've been devising a plan to exit from all illegal activity for good. He agreed with my decisions and offered to help me walk a straight line. Momma always said, "A true friend will help you to do positive and better your life and your frenemies are the ones who influence negativity."

Big Mike was a true friend indeed.

Big Mike never knew that I already wrote down his name and federal ID number just in case anything happened to either of us that would get either of us transferred. I planned to stay in touch with Big Mike. One day in the recreation yard, Big Mike gave me his ID so that I could sign out a medicine ball and a jump rope from the rec resource center. His ID read Michael Mitchell, 10013-007. Big Mike's fed number was as old as the first testament. Mine starts with "5".

Big Mike spoke with excitement about how he earned his G.E.D, completed carpentry class, anger management class and the Challenge Program as well. The Challenge Program is a program for inmates who are willing to make a positive change in life. It's something like a life skills/problem solving course. Being that Big Mike has those credentials to take with him, when he does in front of the parole commission, he felt that his chances of being released outweighed his chances of being turned down on a Libra scale. I personally thought so, too.

On October 21, 2016, Michael Mitchell AKA Big Mike was granted his wish. The U.S. Parole Commission recommended his release and when his action sheet, which showed the final decision, came back through the mail to him that November, he had a release date set for August 18th 2017. Our case manager, Ms. Vank, immediately put together Big Mike's halfway house package to get him a date. That December, Ms. Vank gave Big Mike an early Christmas present. His halfway house date was set for February 17th 2017, approximately one month after mine. Big Mike was issued six months of halfway house and a lifetime full of freedom.

CHAPTER 13

"I'm out this bitch!" I yelled out loud as I walked out the front doors

of FCI Cumberland. It felt as if I was being released from the gates of

hell. I was given a 12 hour furlough to get to Hope Village halfway

house in Southeast, DC. I had to be there by 8pm.

Tanya took the day off from work and dropped Little Bo over to spend the night at my mom's house the night before. Tanya wanted to make sure that she made it to pick me up on time so my mother made sure Little Bo made it to school on time this morning. She was looking beautiful and sexy as always. Tanya was waiting in the parking lot, leaning her behind on the front hood of our Mercedes. She was dressed in a sky blue L.L. Bean jacket that stopped at her waist line above her hips to show her sexy shape in my white polo pajama pants, which looked good as hell hugging her ass. I walked to her and immediately shared saliva as we held each other. After about a minute, Tanya jiggled her sexy ass around the car to get in the driver's seat. The way her ass moved let me know she wasn't wearing any panties. Tanya drove 80 miles per hour the entire ride, confirming my allegations. We got home in less than two hours. As soon as we walked inside our home, she aggressively tore away my clothing.

Tanya was like a mad woman in a cat fight. We kissed and stripped each other's clothing away to the bedroom. By the time I was in my bed, I was asshole naked wearing socks only, with my manhood inside of Tanya's mouth and my tongue inside of her womanhood. We performed a 69 position for about 10 to 15 minutes.

I bust my first nut within the first three, and then another one no more than ten minutes later. Tanya had about three orgasms herself. I then lifted Tanya's vagina out of my mouth and flipped her over onto her back, sexing her in missionary position for about another 20 minutes.

Tanya was screaming, "Fuck me! Fuck me! Fuck me Daddy!" over and over and over. She sounded like one of my mother's old scratched up New Edition records. I can't lie, that's what motivated me to pound the pussy harder. Tanya was screaming so in tune that I thought she could have been a hook to a new Luke track. I finally bust my last nut before rolling over and immediately falling asleep. I was out cold. When Tanya decided to wake me up it was two o'clock in the afternoon. She had drove to Pizza Boli's and all to get some pizza while I rested.

After I ate a few slices of pizza and immediately took a shit afterwards, Tanya instructed me to hurry up and get myself together so that I could ride with her to pick up Little Bo from school. She said all he kept talking about yesterday was about his daddy coming home. She also said that he called her phone at 5 o'clock this morning asking her if she was up and ready to go pick up his daddy. Little Bo missed me a lot and I missed him more.

I grabbed my underclothes out of my dresser drawer and went to grab a towel, washcloth and some black soap from the linen closet. I wasn't inside of the shower for more than 15 minutes before I got out, lotioned my skin, put on my Degree deodorant and my Cool Water body oil, followed by my black G-Star hoodie and my grey 993 New Balance shoes. I then topped off my outfit with a grey and black San Antonio Spurs fitted cap. It was at that point that I realized that it was about time for me to go clothes shopping. I had gained about ten pounds of muscle in the feds. The jeans I had on were feeling kind of small. I am definitely not the skinny jean type of guy and don't ever plan to become one. Relax fit only and these were not relaxing. After I stuck my arms into my black L.L Bean jacket, I glanced at the clock on the wall which read 3:05pm. Tanya and I hurried out of the front door in a rush to go pick Little Bo up from school.

It was 3:25pm when we pulled up and parked by the front door of his school. Ron Brown Middle School! I remember when I went to this school when I was younger. At that time it was called Roper Middle School. After no more than 3 minutes of waiting, I saw Little Bo walking out of the school, jumping in the air in a shooting basketball motion, talking to another little boy who attended the school. "These kids are so tiny." I mumbled to myself. 'Was I this small?' I thought before Tanya backhand slapped my arm in excitement as she pointed to Little Bo with a big smile on her face as she said,

"There go your little man right there."

I immediately opened the car door and stepped out on the sidewalk and slowly walked over to Little Bo, while he stood near the flag pole talking to his friend about what seemed to be basketball. When I got within 50 feet of Lil Bo he turned his head toward my direction in reaction, initially not noticing who was approaching and turned back and faced his friend. It was like in a second a lightning bolt shot through Lil Bo because he quickly snapped his head back toward me with his eyes as big as softballs when he realized it was me approaching him. His face lit up with joy before yelling, "Daddy!" He then ran toward me and wrapped his arms around my waist as I hugged and kissed him on his forehead.

"I love you Little Bo." I said to my little son, holding back tears of joy.

"I love you too daddy, but I'ma beat you up for leaving me." Little Bo said as he threw his ineffective punches to my body. I curled up and laughed before I slowly jogged toward the car while Little Bo chased behind me still swinging his punches. When we reached the car, he hopped in the back seat and I sat in the back with him. We threw harmless punches the entire ride to our house. When we got inside of our home, we wrestled around for a while before having a father and son talk. I had some catching up to do. We talked about sports, his so-called girlfriend and his good grades at school until it was time for me to head to the halfway house.

We pulled over on the corner of Ainger and Langston Place at 7:23pm. Even though it only took 15 minutes to get there from my apartment, I decided to get there a little earlier to leave a good impression about myself. I learned that that's how you keep the authorities off your back. That fake hardcore, "I don't give a damn" attitude was played out. We're in the generation of thinkers. After showing my love to Little Bo and Tanya and vice versa, I then strolled down the hill of Langston Place to building 20. After being buzzed into the apartment building, I walked into the staff administration office where I signed in and was issued a bed robe and a room number. Room 102 was my temporary domain. When I walked into the apartment style room, I saw three people sitting in the living room area on couches watching a Washington Wizard's basketball game.

I introduced myself and greeted the three men with a hand shake.

"My name Trap and I be around Minnesota Avenue by Mario's Pizza place." The younger guy said, who looked to be about 21. The other two looked like there were no older than 30 apiece.

"My name Juve, holmes, I be around Clay Terrace." The dark skinned guy with dreadlocks said.

"My name Lou, bruh, I'm from da Heights." The clean cut, big lipped guy said last.

"So you from Lincoln Heights?" I asked.

"Yea, that's where I be. You know people up there?" Lou asked me.

"No doubt, I'm from Cruddy Island." I replied.

"Oh that's what's up. Go 'head and get yourself together, we got all day tomorrow to rap, bruh."

"True." I responded to Lou as I walked into one of the two bedrooms. The room I walked into had four beds in the form of two bunk-beds.

Only one of the three beds had a blanket on it, which let me know

that the other three were vacant. I proceeded to place the sheets and

blanket on the bed that I claimed, the bottom bunk located directly

across from the already occupied bottom bunk bed. I finished

making up my bed and then went to sit out in the front room with the

fellas and watched the rest of the basketball game, while we all bonded

and got acquainted with one another. It was no secret that Trap and

Juve were high as giraffe pussy and Lou was twisted like a high ankle

sprain. I could smell the alcohol reeking out of the deer park water

bottle between every sip. To me, they all seemed like some cool

dudes which made me feel comfortable with calling it a night

immediately after the Wizard's game ended. The three of them sat

out in the front room conversing while I chased a dream.

CHAPTER 14

The next day I met with my case manager and job counselor. Before that, I awoke to see that Lou was my roommate. I really thought about placing a sign on our room door that said, "LOU ROOM!" After dismissing the thought, I called Tanya from a pay phone that was located in the hallway of the building. I instructed her to put together some outfits, underclothes, shoes, cosmetics, a towel and washcloth and bring it to me after she left work. I also informed her about my 72 hour blackout. For the first three days I was not authorized to go anywhere outside of the halfway house campus, only to building 28, which was the cafeteria and back to my building.

The loud speaker broadcasted, "JOB TRAINING CLASSES AREA AT 1:00PM IN BUILDING 44 COME ON OVER!" she said, "COME ON OVER!" like she was inviting us to an open session of her kitty cat. I thought to myself, 'Damn, I need to get over there ASAP,' at least until I finally saw the face behind the microphone. A white lady that was too damn old with a body built like a bag of flour. BUSTED! Something I couldn't enjoy in the free world unless I was just mentally ill, desperate or on medication or something.

Later that day, Tanya brought me my belongings just like I asked her. For the next few days I was confined to Hope Village. More than enough time for me to get my mind set on my next move. Monday morning was here, and I participated in my job counselor, Ms. Stokes', job preparation session which didn't take more than an hour. Afterwards, she issued me a four hour travel pass after I plead to her about how I desperately needed a haircut. She understood and agreed to give me a pass that was from 11AM to 3PM. I went straight to the barbershop to get groomed. For the next few months while I was still in the halfway house I pretty much kept the same routine. I promptly got in touch with my connects, Jay and Marty. They were ready to resume where we left off, but I did let them know that due to my current situation things were going to be ran a little differently and slower, at least until I got out of the halfway house. They understood and agreed to the process and respected my decision.

I was purchasing the same way as far as quantity but not the same way as far as time. One day of work became two. I later found out that my partner Nate was fucking Ms. Stokes, which made my situation so much better. He told her that we were family and to look out for me and she definitely did so. She would give me day passes from 9AM to 6PM Monday through Friday and would give me eight hour passes for Saturday and Sundays. I would exercise at least one hour every morning from Monday to Saturday and took Sundays off to relax my body.

Kalvin and Conrad would pick me up once in a while to take me out to eat, and treated me to clothes shopping one day. Once in a while I would drive my Kia Sorrento up to the halfway house and park in Woodland, a housing project located directly across the street from Hope Village. My partner named Charlie lived around there as well and he would look after my truck whenever needed. I had too many friends with vehicles for me to risk a violation and get sent back to prison. I had no problem with hopping on the public metro bus or train. Sometimes I would even catch a cab. About a month after I was in the halfway house, Big Mike was released from the prison to their custody.

On majority of his day passes, he would spend his time with his wife, Sonya. Big Mike was housed in building 50. Even though we were in different buildings, we would still find time to kick it with each other. I would go up to his building or sometimes he would chill down at mine. Most of the time we spent would be in the chow hall if we were there during meal times. A month after Big Mike was in the halfway house, he had developed a new glow on his face. He was like a lion being released from the zoo. You could see the freedom in his swag, aura and demeanor compared to the institutionalized stroll and mean mug. The wonderful things freedom and pussy can do for a man. I was happy for him. I had to update Big Mike on the dress code and he took no time to pick up on it. I had to tell him, "No more 90's drop socks!" Big Mike chose the wise route.

He kept his style basic and grown man. Mostly Polo style clothing.
You can't lose with that. The day before I was being released from
the halfway house, I was walking down the hill of Langston Place after
being dropped off at the bus stop on Ainger Place. It was one o'clock
and I had decided to get back early. I saw Big Mike playing it close as
he was directly across from the street from Hope Village on Reynolds
Place, sitting on the hood of a car and kissing his wife, Sonya. It's
policy that we are not allowed to be riding in vehicles unless reported
to the administration and from past conversations with Big Mike, I
knew he always told them that he catches the metro bus or train to get
more time on his pass for travel.

So like the good friend that I am, if I see you falling it's my duty to
catch you. "Big Mike!" I yelled across the street to Big Mike.

"What's up, Lou, you aight?" Big Mike asked me with a concerned
look on his face.

"Yeah, I'm good big homie but you slipping!" I responded.

"Huh? What you talking 'bout, Lou?" Big Mike asked, his
expression now showing confusion.

"You know these people be geeking and shit," I yelled to him in a hush tone as I proceeded to walk toward him before continuing, "All it takes is for one of them pressed ass counselors to walk or ride past and assume that you just got out of that car. Tighten up, big guy." I said with a smirk on my face. Big Mike burst out laughing as he looked at his wife and then back at me.

 "No B-shit, champ. I am loafing, but she worth every slice, ya dig me." Big Mike said, still laughing. He then gave his wife a goodbye kiss before she got inside of her car and started the engine. Big Mike began walking in my direction as Sonya pulled off, honking her horn and waving at Big Mike and me. From where I stood, Sonya looked like a beautiful woman. She was high yellow with black hair. Sonya was driving an up-to-date, dark blue, two door Acura. "What's up, Lou, where you coming from?" Big Mike asked me as we fist bumped hands.

 "You know me, tryna get it off the ground, back to da money." I replied.

 "Oh yea! Man don't forget about me, bruh!" I said as we fist bumped again before separating.

 "You outta here tomorrow right?" Big Mike asked.

"Yeah, I'm ghost."

"Aight then, I'ma make sure I call you to keep a check up on you."

"Yeah make sure you do that and just let me know if you need anything and I'll make sure you get it."

"Aight then, that's a bet."

"Aight big homie."

"Love you Slim."

"Love you too Pimpin'." I responded as I proceeded to walk into the halfway house. I returned early for a couple of reasons.

Reason one, I needed to pack the remainder of my property and get ready to depart from the halfway house tomorrow morning. I didn't have a whole lot to pack being that I already started taking things home a couple of days prior but I didn't want to be packing later on tonight, either. I wanted to give myself enough time to relax my mind and prepare myself for a greater schedule. Reason two, you could call me superstitious, but I really came in early because of the bad luck that I be having sometimes. Right before I got out of the halfway house, something bad was bound to happen. Something stupid and careless always happens when good things are about to happen if you place yourself in a bad environment or situation. I know the life I was living and I didn't mind walking on eggshells.

I saw too many sudden surprises in life to not be a little paranoid. I call it wisdom. I was getting older and wise to the cause and effects of life, especially the streets. It was time to use what God gave me, "A brain!"

CHAPTER 15

It's 2018, and I've been out of the halfway house for a year now and business couldn't have been any better. About three months after my release from the halfway house, Big Mike also got released and it was like he was working for Wall Street. The hustle and clientele he had was loyal. At times, I thought he was buying all the work for himself. I was doubling up on everything that I was purchasing. 50 pounds of mid-grade turned into 100, 25 pounds of loud pack turned into 50 and 5,000 e-pills turned into 10,000. This shit was turning into a career, something that I didn't want. Tanya and I placed a down payment on a 2016 Mercedes-Benz Sprinter van for our vacations and were contemplating on upgrading the 2012 CLS63 however decided against our thoughts since we were also house shopping as well as engaged.

I proposed to Tanya in Manhattan, New York at the New Year's Eve 2017 ball drop countdown. Everything was perfect timing. As soon as the ten second countdown started, I began to propose as the crowd was yelling,

"HAPPY NEW YEAR!"

I could see Tanya's lips moving, saying, "Yes! Yes! Yes!" before we passionately kissed.

Big Mike and Sonya joined Tanya and I for a week-long vacation in New York. We had to reserve our rooms at The Carter Hotel three months in advance since all of the five stars were sold out. We were able to see the New York Times newspaper building that was just across the street. We left DC and drove to New York City one week in advance, which should have been two, just to get into the city. Traffic was at its worst around this time of year. Even though the experience was perfect, I doubt if I'd ever do that again. That's what you call a "once in a lifetime" experience. Big Mike and I had been doing too much splurging and partying to my liking. Being that I'm a low key, out of the way type of person, clubbing twice a month was way too much for me. Big Mike had me in Go-Go clubs with Big G and the Backyard Band, at the Go-Go awards, the DMV awards and all type of shit.

He had threw a five star birthday bash at Stadium Nightclub slash strip club. He had arranged performances by Fat Trel, Shy Glizzy, Bigg Dabb, Top Dolla Sweizy, Lola Monroe with Dre all Day hosting the function. Big Mike bought himself a silver 2012 A8 Audi and rented out an orange Bugatti from some multi-millionaire friend he had met in the feds for his birthday weekend. It was Big Mike's 40th birthday and I didn't plan to be a party pooper, but I did inform him on how much attention he was bringing to our small operation.

I could tell by the expression on his face that he wasn't feeling my comments although he acknowledged respect of them. Even though Big Mike did extravagant things for his birthday, I was reluctant to do the same for mine—at least not for the crowd to see. In celebration of my 30th birthday, I decided to keep it grown man since that's what I was now. Big Mike, Sonya, Tanya and I all went on a double date out on a yacht that we had rented out for a few hours from some guy at my mom's church. First, we started with dinner at Tony & Joe's Seafood restaurant and then rode the yacht to the National Harbor, Maryland before spending the remainder of the night on crap tables and at slot machines at the MGM Grand. We then crashed out at the Gaylord Hotel for two days, which was a relaxing and romantic adventure for me, courtesy of Tanya.

One night, about two months ago, Big Mike and I almost engaged in a fist fight. Big Mike called my phone around 1 o'clock in the morning, sounding paranoid as hell. I then hopped out of my bed from Tanya as Big Mike plead for me to come bail him out not from jail, but from an altercation. He said that he was trapped in one of the rooms at the Residence Inn, Marriott Hotel in Lanham, Maryland. He said that some guys were trying to rob him and possibly kill him. He said that they were sitting inside of a car in the parking lot beside his car. Big Mike told me his room number and I disconnected our call and let Tanya know what was going on. I immediately got dressed, grabbed my two .40 caliber, SIG Sauer handguns and zoomed out of the house. I hit about 90 miles per hour down route 450, to bail Big Mike out of some bullshit. When I pulled into the parking lot, all I could think of was when my late friend Snead called me to pick him up from this hotel back in 2009. As soon as I pulled into the parking lot, Snead was running toward my car with a flat screen TV, which he stole from the hotel, cradled inside of his arms like an oversized baby. After having a brief laugh at my thoughts, I snapped back to the matter at hand. I slow paced through the parking lot, surveying my surroundings as I looked for Big Mike's Audi.

When I spotted its location I cruised past it, taking notice of vehicles parked in the vicinity in which there were none. I figured they were either inside of the hotel or had left already. After parking, I placed one of my SIGs into my body wrap waist holster. It wrapped my body like a girdle. I then placed the other SIG under my driver seat before reaching into the backseat to recover my tactical 550 windbreaker jacket, put it on and zipped it closed. I was war ready.

I walked inside of the hotel and rode the elevator up to the 4th floor. I walked up to room 414, placed my ear to the door and then lightly knocked before standing on the side of the room doorway with the .40 caliber in my hand, behind my back. "Who's that?" Big Mike yelled from inside of the room.

"A ghost, mothafucka, now open the door." I replied in a mellow tone, looking behind me down the hallway to make sure no one was there. Big Mike opened the room door and the room was dark as midnight.

"They was tryna get me, Lou." Big Mike said, as I walked inside of the room behind him.

"Who?" I asked, placing my SIG Sauer into my body holster.

"Them!" Big Mike yelled. Blankets flew from the bed and the bathroom door flew open simultaneously, shining light into the dark hotel room and displaying four naked women, ass and titties everywhere! Two were under the blankets of the double beds and the other two came storming out of the bathroom toward me as they grabbed and pushed me onto the bed.

I instinctively stiff armed the women to stop their pursuit of doing whatever they were planning to do to me. I instantly hopped up from the bed while Big Mike clicked on the lamp light that was mounted on the wall.

"What the fuck!" I said, as I created space between myself and the women. I then took a couple of steps backwards towards the doorway, giving Big Mike a deep stare of anger, distrust and frustration.

"What's up, lil bruh?" Big Mike asked, as he threw his hands up in the air out of frustration.

"Fuck you mean, what's up?" I spat at Big Mike as the four females

huddled together on the bed behind Big Mike on the opposite side of

the room from where I stood. "Nigga you called me out of my bed

with my wife for some dumb ass, anything bitches. I thought a nigga

was tryna kill you, slim. You on some wild nigga shit, foreal!" I yelled

to Big Mike.

"Nigga please," Big Mike said, as he waved his hand towards me like

he was swatting down my words before continuing, "First of all, she

isn't your wife yet and second, you need to loosen up and get some

different pussy for once. I'm tryna show you a good fuckin' time, got

damn!"

"Nigga fuck you!" I spat at Big Mike, making him take a couple steps

in my direction before stepping and spreading his arms wide.

"Fuck me, huh? That's how you feel Lou, fuck me?" Big Mike said.

"Yea nigga! Here I'm still on papers just like you, plus I'm a registered gun offender!" I said to Big Mike and then continued, "You ain't think about that, huh? Only if your dick had a brain you would've been a modern Einstein! And nigga ain't you fuckin' married?! I bet you ain't got no rubbers!" I said, waiting for Big Mike to show me a condom but instead he once again swatted his hand at me as he turned toward the bed and sat down.

 "Slim gone 'bout your business champ before we fall out about nothin'." Big Mike said, sounding exhausted.

 "Yea, you right!" I sarcastically replied, nodding my head up and down in agreement before reaching for the door handle. I turned to Big Mike as I opened the room door and said, "Don't wait 'til you see clouds before saving for a rainy day." I then turned and walked out of the room.

"What the fuck is that supposed to mean?" I heard Big Mike mumble as the door closed behind me. I learned that every question doesn't warrant a response. If a person used thought they would get their answer every time. When I got back home I lied to Tanya about what had went down at the hotel that night because I didn't want her to think any different of Big Mike. After that episode, Big Mike and I didn't spend as much time with each other as we usually did. Business continued as scheduled and honestly, I think I liked it better that way. Even though I missed the fun times we had together as friends, I felt that if we planned for it to last a long time, it was best if we created space between each other. I saved a lot more money and from the look of Big Mike's purchases, he was saving a lot more, also. Everything happens for a reason. At the end of the day, it was for the better.

CHAPTER 16

"Little Bo, hurry your little ass up boy!" I yelled towards the bathroom to Little Bo as he was brushing his teeth and washing his face. "You can take your time and miss the bus if you want to, I damn sure won't be taking you to no Pennsylvania. It'll be one boring summer for you!" I said as I placed Little Bo's gym bags filled with his clothes, hygiene products and whatever else he had in there by the front door.

"I'm coming now, old man!" Little Bo yelled back to me from the bathroom, laughing at his own comment. Little Bo always got a kick out of calling me "old man". I can admit that I did have a few specks of grey hairs on my head, and since he'd discovered them a couple of years ago in the visiting hall of Cumberland, he'd been riding my coat tail ever since. "Old man" this and "old man" that, and I was even starting to feel a little slower. One day, I went to play Little Bo in a one-on-one game of basketball and he flew right by me on the court, like I was a statue. He made this young age of thirty inherit ten extra years.

"I'ma take your bags down to the car. We got thirty minutes to be there so hurry up, and lock the door when you come out!" I yelled to him as I opened the front door before lifting one of his gym bags onto my shoulders by the strap and grabbing the other two, one in each hand. After placing the gym bags inside of the truck of my CLS63, I walked back to the building, wondering where Little Bo was. As soon as I pulled open the building door, I saw Little Bo stepping off of the elevator, basketball in hand. "Bring your little ass on!" I yelled, waving my hand and signaling for him to hurry up as I turned around and walked towards my car and sat inside. Little Bo ran out of the building, bouncing his basketball twice before flopping into the passenger seat. "Now you gonna be late. I wanted to grab you some'n to eat for breakfast before you took that ride." I said to Little Bo with frustration in my tone. I then started the car before zooming out of the parking lot, hoping to catch the bus in time. Little Bo was on his way to sports camp. He had been going there for the past three years, courtesy of my mom. The camp had multiple sports departments, and Little Bo was signed up for their basketball program. He had just graduated from middle school two weeks ago. He was committed to starting his first year in high school at Cesar

Chavez Public Charter School in Northwest next school year.

Little Bo had plenty of high school choices and offers on the table but decided to attend Cesar Chavez so that he could continue to play basketball with his best friend, Malik. Malik outsourced Little Bo in their middle school championship game against Jefferson Middle School. Brown, defeated Jefferson 62 to 30 in which Little Bo scored 16 points, 12 assists and 1 steal, but still came up short to win the championship MVP to Malik who had scored 33 points and had 8 pounds in which 6 of them rebounds, were offensive. Malik dominated the boards. Little Bo took it pretty well though. Better than expected.

I figured that since he was named the MVP of the league and the fact that it was his best friend Malik who had won the award over him that helped the fault be ineffective. Honestly, Little Bo seemed championship MVP which spoke volumes about his character. I was glad to see my son didn't inherit a coward's trait, "HATE". The camp that Little Bo was attending was in Kutztown, Pennsylvania at Kutztown University. It's called the FCA camp. FCA stands for Fellowship of Christian Athletes. Little Bo is scheduled to be there for four weeks. The program's staff are Christian men and women who are or were high school, college, AAU or professional sports coaches, executives, trainers or athletes themselves. Last summer, Little Bo took a picture with Tim Tebow, who was on the campus assisting with the football program.

Little Bo's game was by far advanced, and that program seemed like it helped his mechanics, as well as his character, mature. He was ranked no. 30 on the Nation's Top 100 Basketball Prospects list as well as 4th in the nation for point guards before even playing one game of high school basketball. I can't lie, Little Bo was the truth. His season average was 18 points, 7 rebounds, 9 assists and 2 steals per game. He had Oak Hill Academy, Dematha, Gonzaga, Dunbar High School and many more mailing letters and brochures to our house. They were camping out in our parking lot, even going as far as harassing my mother in church, trying to bribe us into accepting their offers for Little Bo to attend their school programs. Little Bo made his own choice and I supported his decision. Besides, Cesar Chavez has a great academic curriculum as well as sports program which they don't get much credit for. Don't get me wrong, basketball is cool, but not first priority.

Little Bo had to learn something first. We stopped at the McDonalds on New York Avenue by Club Ibiza to grab Little Bo something to eat. He ordered two steak bagels, two hash browns and a large orange juice. After receiving his food, I sped out of the McDonald's drive-thru and three minutes later I parked on N Street in Northwest directly in front of Dunbar High School.

There were about thirty cars parked around the school with people resting inside of them waiting for the buses to pull up. We had arrived ten minutes before scheduled departure but were on time because after about four or five minutes of waiting, two buses were turning onto N Street. All of the vehicles that were parked directly in front of the school began moving out of the way making space for the buses to park. After the buses were stationed, we all loaded the bottom of the buses with luggage. While everyone was saying their goodbyes to their loved ones, the bus operator yelled, "ALL ABOARD!"

Five minutes later, the buses were loaded and departing.

I went straight back to the house to catch up on some needed sleep. It was only 6:30 in the morning, so I figured I could get me at least two more hours of Z's. When I arrived in the house, Tanya was already up, getting herself ready for work. While driving home, I started thinking to myself and decided that today would be the perfect day to transition my life for the better. I made the decision to have a talk with Big Mike. Little Bo had a promising future and I wanted to make sure that I was around to experience it.

CHAPTER 17

When I awoke from my nap, I glanced over to the clock that was sitting on my nightstand. It read 10:44 AM. I had slept a little longer than I had planned, but I wasn't upset because Lord knows I needed the rest. I reached for my phone to check my voice messages and then checked my text messages and saw that Big Mike had text me at 9:13 AM. His text said to call his phone when I got the message, so I proceeded to do so. We agreed to meet up at one o'clock that afternoon in the parking lot of Circle 7 Express, a convenience store located around my neighborhood. After cooking myself some breakfast and eating, I took a shit, shaved and then showered.

It was a little after 12:30 PM when I finished, so I shot out of the front door on my way to meet Big Mike. My white G-Shock read 12:58 PM when I pulled into the corner store parking lot. I circled through the lot, surveying the cars and the people inside of them, seeing no sign of Big Mike. I then settled into a parking space on the side of the convenience store.

I then got out of my truck and walked inside of the store to grab myself a bottle of vitamin water and some peanut M&M's. I approached the counter, digging in my pocket to retrieve my cash. "What's up, Lou?" a soft, mellow females voice said, as I was unfolding the cash that I was holding. It was the voice of June, a 40 year old mixed breed woman who lived around my hood. "Two thirty-nine." She said, before I handed her a five dollar bill. I then waved my hand gesturing for her to keep the change. "I'm cooling, what you 'bout to do?" June asked.

"Nothing yet. Probably run a couple errands, that's about it." I replied.

"Oh yea. Well—"

"Lou!" A loud voice yelled from the front entrance of the store, interrupting the conversation between June and I. The voice belonged to Chugaloo Roc, who was standing in the doorway and waving his hand for me to come toward him, while Lil' X stood outside of the store holding the door and waving his hand also. Chugaloo Roc and Lil' X were products of Jmo.

I didn't know the two of them very well but respected them because they were Jmo's little brothers.

"What's up, y'all?" I asked in a concerned voice.

"Come holla at us real quick." Chugaloo Roc said before walking out of the store.

"Aye June, I'ma holla at you later, aight?" I said to June as I walked out of the store to see what Chugaloo Roc and Lil' X were so anxious to talk about. I shook both of their hands before I began to walk toward my truck. Chugaloo Roc and Lil' X followed while shaking their heads from left to right. "What the hell wrong with you niggaz?" I asked.

"Oh you must not be hipped?" Chugaloo Roc replied.

"Hipped about what?" I asked as we stopped in front of my truck while I leaned my rear end on the front hood.

"You just got saved from Master Splinter. Now let me hold

some'n?" Lil' X said while laughing.

"Master Splinter? Who you talking 'bout, June?" I asked in

confusion.

"Yea, shawty wicked. That bitch fish grease, bruh." Chugaloo Roc

replied.

"Whose case she on?"

"Big bruh case, JMO case." Chugaloo Roc said.

"She testified during his trial and all." Lil' X added. As we stood in

the parking lot of the store they gave me the entire scoop. We

conversed for about five minutes before I saw Big Mike pull into the

parking lot before parking in a space next to my truck.

"Aye y'all, this me right here. I gotta run, but we gonna chop it up

later on 'bout this situation. I know it's true because of certain shit

y'all said, but I'ma rap to y'all later about shawty." I said as I fist

bumped Chugaloo Roc and Lil' X, before waving my hand in the air

to get Big Mike's attention and climbing in my truck.

Big Mike then rolled down his front passenger side window.

"What's up?" Big Mike said.

"Come get in. Ride with me real quick, bruh." I responded. After rolling up his windows, shutting off the engine and locking the doors of his Audi, Big Mike then climbed into the front passenger seat of my truck while I waited in the driver's seat with the engine running. I then pulled onto I-295, going towards Kenilworth Avenue. Five minutes later, we pulled up to an abandoned warehouse on Frolich Lane in Hyattsville, Maryland.

"What the hell is this?" Big Mike asked in confusion.

"Just what it look like, now get out." I said as I shut off the engine, got out of my truck and walked toward the abandoned building. Big Mike slow paced behind me, looking at the building before asking,

"What's this about?"

"Our future." I replied. The frail wooden door to the building made a loud screeching noise as I opened it. With Big Mike trailing behind me, I then walked deeper into the warehouse before stopping in a big open space with my hands stretched out wide like Jesus being crucified. I then slowly spun around and did a 180 while looking around at the building before looking at Big Mike, who stood 10 feet away. "You see this? This here is our future big dawg. I'ma buy this building and we're gonna own this property." I said to Big Mike as he nodded his head up and down, acknowledging what I was saying.

"Okay, I like where this is going. Finish." Big Mike said.

"At the time I'm like a rock stuck in a hard place. I can't decide between opening a night spot or a multi-shop."

"What the hell is a multi-shop?" Big Mike calmly asked.

"I'm glad you asked. Now see my vision." I said as I looked toward the ceiling and then continued, "Fresh & Clean Grooming Center. A barber shop slash beauty salon, laundromat slash dry cleaning spot, car wash slash car detailing. And check this out, you can even bring your little ugly ass Yorkie to get groomed at our pet grooming center. I mean, fresh means success, feel me?" I said, hysterically and convincing, sounding like a bubble gum commercial.

Big Mike stood where he stood with his arms crossed, shaking his head up and down with a grinning smile on his face which confirmed that he saw my vision as well. "So where do I come into play at?" he asked.

"Come on big homie, you know you with me every step of the way." I replied.

"I understand where you coming from, but I don't know how to do nothing but carpentry, which I learned in the feds."

"And?"

"I mean, I don't know shit about building a business." Big Mike said with frustration in his voice.

"So does that mean that you can't learn? I mean, I do believe that the late and great Titanic was built by professionals, which sunk. The internationally known Ark, compliments of my man Noah, was built by amateurs and lasted as long as the NBA playoffs." I said, as I stared into the eyes of Big Mike, waiting for a response.

"I feel you home team. I'm with you, but what about what we got going on now?"

"What about it, Mikey?"

"I'm saying, we chewing heavy, champ."

"And that's all cool, but that's just for now. This is forever." I said as I took a few steps towards Big Mike, stopping when we were arm distance apart. "Look here, bruh. Stopping while you're ahead is not the same as quitting, feel me?" I said. Big Mike's face frowned up as his eyes began to wander as if he was trying to catch a thought in his head.

"Who said that?" Big Mike asked.

"What you mean who said that? I just said that." I replied, trying to hold my composure and keep from laughing.

"Naw, nigga, you got that from a movie or some'n." Big Mike said while smiling.

"Yea, yea whatever you just hating." I said as I walked past Big Mike to the doorway. He jokingly pushed the back of my shoulder when I walked past him.

"Yea, whatever nigga." He paused. "Aye Lou." He added, making me stop and turn to face him. When I looked at him he was rubbing his right shoulder with his left hand while rotating his arm in a swing motion like Cam Newton does before game time.

"You aight big homie?" I asked.

"Yea I'm good my nigga. I got shot in this shoulder back in the day.

It always aches when it's 'bout to rain." Big Mike said, before taking a

brief pause and continuing, "That ain't what I stopped you for though.

I just wanted to apologize about that night at the hotel. I realized I

placed your life in jeopardy over some pussy. Wrong is wrong and

right is right. I just..."

 "Hold up big homie," I intervened. "That's some old shit, bruh.

We ain't gonna reach back and you don't owe me a damn thing but

your loyalty. Small things to a giant, ya dig. Now let's get up out here

before that asbestos shit get us sick." I said to Big Mike before we

walked out of the warehouse.

 While driving, I explained to Big Mike how the warehouse is going

to be one of our three pick-up and drop-off spots until the

development begins. As soon as the construction begins, the game is

over for me. I also told him that he needed to go and see a physical

therapist for that shoulder. After dropping Big Mike off to his car, I

called him to let him know to meet me at the warehouse, which I

nicknamed "The Groom" at five o'clock. As I drove down the

highway it started pouring down raining, like Big Mike predicted. I

guess his bones don't lie. I had always thought that was a myth.

CHAPTER 18

Later that day, after meeting up with Big Mike at the "Groom Spot",

I then followed him to one of his stash houses at Oakcrest Towers, an

apartment community on Brooks Drive in Forestville, Maryland.

That was Big Mike's hideout spot from the wifey, when they had their

fall outs. He had this dark chocolate stripper female, named Dark

China, living there.

I met Dark China before and had socialized with her several times.

I can honestly say that for her to be a dancer at a high maintenance

and baller filled club like The Stadium DC, she showed a lot of

loyalty towards Big Mike.

I mean, after work she would go straight home like she had a government, nine to five job. She was a true home body woman, and catered to my partner Big Mike hand and feet. I had to take my hat off to the big homie. He played down law properly.

The rain had stopped about 2 hours ago. It threw down for a strong two and a half hours nonstop, and you better bet your bottom dollar Big Mike hit me with the, "told you so," when we had met at the Groom Spot. As the clouds parted, the sun shined harder through them as they separated.

The ground was drying pretty quickly. Big Mike went inside of his stash house as I sat in my truck waiting outside of the building. No more than five minutes later, Big Mike re-appeared in the building doorway walking out of the building towards my truck. While he climbed into the front seat my phone rang. It was my big cousin, Vell.

"Hello?" I spoke into the phone.

"What's up lil' cuz, where you at?" Vell asked, sounding as if something was wrong.

"I'm local, what's the verdict?"

"Come through to my house and holla at me real quick, it's important."

"Aight then, gimme 'bout fifteen, twenty minutes."

"Aight, I'll be here."

"Cool." I said before ending the call.

"What's up? Everything good?" Big Mike asked out of concern. I guess he noticed the puzzled look on my face.

"Yea I think so." I replied as I shifted my gear into drive. "That was my cousin Vell. He asked me to slide past his house to holler at him real quick. You got some'n to do?" I asked Big Mike.

"Naw bruh, I'm with you. Go handle your business." He replied.

"That's a bet." I said as I pulled out of the parking lot, headed to Vell's house. On our way there, Big Mike and I discussed going bowling later. I could tell that he was feeling some type of way about my comment about him needing physical therapy. I guess he wanted to prove to me that he can still activate that shoulder. The older people get, it seems as though they feel that they always have to prove themselves to a younger person, especially physically! I considered letting Big Mike win a game or two later, just to keep his confidence level high. When I pulled into the complex of Vell's house all of the parking spaces in the parking lot were full, so I parked my truck alongside a curb at the far end of the parking lot, directly across from Vell's front door.

"What's up, you going in?" I asked Big Mike.

"Naw, that's family business." Replied Big Mike.

"What you mean my nigga, you is family."

"Hahaa! That's what's up. I appreciate the love lil bruh, but I'm good." I'ma chill right here. Go handle yours." Big Mike said, smiling.

"Aight then, gimme 'bout five, ten minutes." I said as I climbed out of my truck.

"Take your time bruh, I ain't got shit to do." Big Mike said as I closed the driver side door. While walking into Vell's yard, I remembered to dodge the gate wire that he never got fixed. When I swung my hand to knock on his door, it flew open before I made any contact.

Vell was standing on the other side nodding his head signaling for me to walk inside. He then closed the door behind me as I walked into his living room, flopping on his black leather sofa. "Aight cuzo, what's the deal pickle?" I said jokingly, as he walked into the living room.

"I need a strap." Vell said with a sad look on his face.

"Nigga please." I spat, before laughing at his comment.

"Foreal though, lil cuz. I need a strap!" Vell said eagerly, calming my laughter.

"For what, cuzo?" I asked.

"'Cause!" He said before taking s brief pause to swallow his saliva. "I been having a lot of dreams lil cuz. A lot of wild ass dreams too. I got killed like three times last week by D-Bo, and in one of my dreams, you killed D-Bo." Vell said sounding nervous.

"In your dream I killed D-Bo?" I replied. "Damn." I said to myself as I took a slight pause to collect my thoughts.

"I'm not saying anything gonna happen but I just need that demonstration just in case I have a situation. Shit be happening." Vell said.

"That's true! When you moving into your new house?"

"In about a couple of months. They still building it out in Charles County, Maryland."

"Oh yeah!" I said excitedly. "You need you a change of scenery anyway. You and that raggedy ass fence that clipped me a few years ago. How's everything at the gym?"

"Mekhi is sharp. Shawty gonna be the next Floyd. He got a weird boxing style but it works for him. He's a natural, and I appreciate your good men Cold Billy and Nate. They've been assisting me in training and mentoring these kids. It's been a blessing."

"You loafing too." I said to Vell. "You ain't got no demonstration 'round here? You gotta always keep you something on stand-by." I said as I stood up and stretched before walking toward the doorway.

"For what? I gave that life up a long time ago. I would've been doing life in prison right now if I kept a pistol around here, especially how much I be telling them youngins to move their asses from in front of my damn house." Vell said as he laughed. "My patience would've been knocked one of their heads off by now."

As I walked out of the door, Vell stood in his doorway laughing before noticing someone in my truck.

"Ain't that your truck right there?" Vell asked, while pointing towards my truck.

"Yea, that's mine." I replied.

"Who's that in your shit?" Vell asked.

"That's Big Mike right there. We done time in the feds together. He good peoples. Been rocking with me since day one." I said, as Vell then waved to Big Mike when he looked in our direction.

"That's what's up." Vell said, as Big Mike waved back acknowledging Vell's greeting.

"You tryna meet him?" I asked Vell, while pointing my thumb toward my truck.

"Nah, not really. Maybe some other time." Vell said while slowly

shaking his head from left to right. "I can't really see him that good

from here, but I can tell he's a big dude." Vell said while giggling.

"Yea, slim a giant." I replied before fist bumping Vell. "But I'ma go

'head and get up on outta' here cuzo."

"Aight, that's a bet. When you gonna bring that through?" Vell

asked, as I walked out of his yard into the parking lot.

"I got you tomorrow cuzo."

"Aight then be safe and love you boy."

"Love you more." I said before climbing into my truck.

"Everything good slim?" Big Mike asked, in concern.

"Yea, everything gucci. Cuzo just on his 'noid shit right now. That

shit come from all of that dirt he done in his past. That shit coming

back to haunt his conscience. That shit start to get to fucking wit' a

nigga when you get older. He'll eventually get over it though." I said

as I laughed while scrolling through my iPhone music playlist.

"Yea it be like that sometimes." Big Mike said while grabbing my

phone out of my hand. "Where's the 'Pac at on here?"

"It's some Makaveli, Me Against The World, Thug Li..."

"Aight, aight, aight, slim I get the picture." Big Mike said before discovering what he'd been looking for.

"Come with me, HAIL MARY nigga!" Big Mike sung aloud with Pac, as I pulled out of the parking lot. "I Ain't No Killa But Don't Push Me, Revenge Is Like The Sweetest Joy Next Ta Getting Pussy!" Big Mike rapped along with 2Pac excitedly before I turned up the volume louder drowning out Big Mike's voice.

The clock on the dashboard read, 7:18PM when I finally found a parking space on 7th and H Street in Northwest. I was parked directly across the street from Gallery Place Metro Station. After I paid for parking through an application on my iPhone, Big Mike and I walked across the street toward Lucky Strike Bowling Lanes in Chinatown. When we bent the corner of a courtyard which leads you into the building of the bowling alley, to my surprise, I saw someone I hadn't seen in a while. Killa Reds! He was walking out of the building with a female friend of his towards our direction. The females was a petite brown skinned woman with a cute face. She was wearing a white halter top, blue jeans, with open toe sandals. She also had pretty long hair. Not bad for Killa Reds. Killa Reds didn't notice me until we got within ten feet from each other. Our eyes immediately locked in on one another as we passed like two red nose pit bulls. Killa Reds had a slight smirk on his face like he took me for a joke.

"Wassup slim." I said, before immediately stopping in my tracks readying myself for attack mode.

"Wassup wit' you slim?" Killa Reds replied, with bass in his voice, as his female friend held him tightly by his elbow.

"Not today please" the female friend pled to Killa Reds.

"Aye Big Mike, wassup wit' your lil homie keep fakin' and shit?" Killa Reds asked.

"Who say he fakin'?" Big Mike replied while shrugging his shoulders.

"Nigga we can work real quick, it's nuttin'" I said, as I took a step towards Killa Reds, before his female friend yanked back his arm and stood in front of him like a human shield.

"No stop it, please sir." The female friend pled to me. "Can you just let it go please?"

Big Mike then stepped from behind me placing his hand on my shoulder restraining me. "Not here lil bruh. There's a time and place for everything." Big Mike said.

"Yea, I'ma catch up wit' you slim." Killa Reds said as he walked off with his female friend.

"Likewise my friend." I replied while being lead towards the building entrance by Big Mike. "And get your bitch feet fixed, her toes ugly as shit!" I yelled, triggering Big Mike to burst into laughter as he yanked me by my shoulder through the doorway of the building.

"Nigga bring your wild ass on." Big Mike said while still laughing at my comment. "Tryna pull a check-in move at the bowling alley and shit."

Though everything seemed so funny at the time being, I had a good feeling that the next time Killa Reds and I crossed paths, it definitely wouldn't be a laughing matter.

CHAPTER 19

It was Saturday morning and the sun was shining high, Tanya opened the blinds to wake me up before she left out of the house because the sun-ray was beaming straight in my face. Every Saturday, Tanya pampered herself at the hair and nail salon and on every other weekend, she would go to a spa to get a massage. I would go to the spa with her like every six months or so. I keep telling myself to make it every three months, but I always get side tracked from my schedule. I was awake for roughly five minutes before my phone rang. When I looked at the screen, it read, BIG MIKE. "Goddamn!" I thought to myself. I haven't heard from him since Wednesday.

After not hearing from him Tuesday, I called to check up with him Wednesday, and he let me know that he's been thinking about our conversation. He said he's been tying up some loose ends and he's working on something, so he can give full contribution to my vision. I must say, I was proud of Big Mike, for recognizing change and taking it upon himself to make something happen. So, I did what a good friend is supposed to do and gave him space. One thing I learned in life is, when a man is putting a plan together, don't crowd his thought pattern with bullshit. Most women don't understand this, that's why I'm with Tanya. She's very open-minded and doesn't crowd my space; she just waits for me.

"Big Mike! Wassup, big homie!" I said jokingly into the phone.

"Ain't too much. What's on your menu today, Lou?" Big Mike asked.

"Well later on, I gotta go holla at Vell for a hot second, then it's whatever." I said.

"You tryna go shoot some pool?"

"It don't matter to me, it's your call bruh."

"Aight then, what time you sliding past cuzo house?"

"Shidd, probably 'bout six or six thirty, some like that, why what's up?"

"Well, I'm tryna see you 'round that time myself, before we go to Galaxy."

"Aight then, that's a bet." I said.

"Same way as Monday." Big Mike said.

"Cool." I said before ending the call. As soon as I got off the phone with Big Mike, I immediately called Vell, to confirm his availability at six o'clock, after he cursed me out about not coming back the following day like agreed, I promised him I would be at his house between six and six thirty, that evening. I got myself together and prepared for a long day. I drove over to my stash apartment in Maryland to gather my drop-offs for the day. I never kept over two pounds of loud or weed at my Northwest apartment. I figured that defeated the purpose of having a second apartment. After prepping everything, I drove around paradise to place the work inside my auntie Wee-Wee house. Wee-Wee wasn't my biological aunt, just a crackhead lady who watched me grow up. I rented out one of her bedrooms at $100 dollars a month just to keep guns and drugs in there. So, I don't have to take the extended risk of driving back and forth from my hood to Maryland. I also do small favors for her such as putting food in her freezer or buy a TV or radio for her apartment. Sometimes, I be thinking, Wee-Wee is really my aunt and I'm sure her feelings are mutual. Once I did my drop off, I chilled around the hood until about a quarter to six. I then grabbed Big Mike's package and drove over to Vell's house. It was a minute after six, when I pulled into his neighborhood parking lot. The lot was full of cars and my normal, secondary parking space had a navy blue Acura parked in it. The windows were tinted, but I could tell that someone was sitting inside. SO, I just double parked in front of Vell's house. I hopped out of my truck and jogged into Vell's yard to knock on his door. Seconds later, Vell opened the door. When I walked inside I removed the pistol from my front right pants pocket as we walked into Vell's living room.

"What the hell is that?" Vell said, as he retrieved .32 revolver from my hand.

"A pistol, cuzo." I replied, while laughing at his comment.

"You sure? I thought that was a cap gun or some'n." Vell joked, while holding the revolver flat in his palm. "Lil cuz, I said I was having nightmares, all this for a dream!" Vell said, trying to control his laughter.

"Aight cuzo, gimme my shit back then." I replied.

"Nah, I'ma keep it, but these youngins playing with thirty shots and better nowadays." Vell said.

"And." I replied.

"And I'ma need 'bout four more of deez." Vell jokingly shouted, which triggered me to laugh harder. "But I guess it'll get the job done temporarily." Vell said, as he shook his head from side to side like he was in shame. "Where the bullets at?" Vell asked, while looking inside the barrel and chamber.

"I got you. I'ma get my clucka' with the VA I.D., and take him to RealCo on Marlboro Pike, tomorrow to grab you a box." I said.

"Goodness lil cuz! You tryna get me killed ain't you?" Vell joked.

"Naw cuzo, I got you." I replied shamefully. "See I had that joint for a minute, in the cut. I ain't never used it before. On the real, you can have that mufucka." I said.

"Sheesh! You tough but I love you though!" Vell said.

"I love you too big cuz." I said as my cell phone rang, pausing our conversation. "Hold up a sec cuzo, let me answer real quick." I said to Vell, as I touched the TALK icon on my phone.

"Wassup big guy?" I said into the phone.

"Wassup where you at now?" Big Mike asked.

"I'm leaving Vell house as we speak on my way to you." I replied while walking toward the front door, placing my hand on the door knob.

"Aight then, I'm just leaving my house, so I guess I'll see you in a lil' bit." Big Mike said.

"Aight, cool, see you soon." I said, ending our call and opening the front door to walk outside. Vell stood behind me in the doorway with the pistol cuffed in his palm.

"I'ma holler at you later, cuzo." I said as I walked toward my truck.

"Aight." Vell responded as an all-black, 2012 Chevy Camaro with some dark ass tints pulled up on me behind my truck and rolled down its windows.

"Bang!" is what the driver of the car yelled out to me. It was Killa Reds with some dread head dude in the passenger seat. "Caught your ass slippin', huh?" Killa Reds said, with a mean mug on his face. If looks could kill, you would have been reading my obituary the next week.

"Aight, work then, nigga and stop horse playing!" I spat at Killa Reds as he switched his gear into reverse.

"Yea you right. Now that I know where you at, I'ma make sure I use my welcome." Killa Reds said.

"Lil' cuz, you aight?" Vell yelled while taking a couple of steps from his doorway toward my direction.

"Oh yea!?" Killa Reds said, eyeing the pistol cuffed in Vell's palm. "I guess he in the game too, huh? I'ma see you niggaz soon!" He finished, simultaneously rolling up his windows and reversing out of the parking lot.

"I'm aight, cuzo." I said to Vell as I climbed into my truck and pulled off. Vell stood on the outside of his yard, watching my truck as I pulled out from in front of his house and onto Montana Avenue. Roughly twenty minutes later, I was pulling into the parking lot of Oakcrest Towers.

When I found a parking space, I sat there with my engine running for about five minutes, replaying the entire Killa Reds situation over in my head. I had to get him out of the way, ASAP. That's when I remembered that Killa Reds was claiming The Nut. I got a partner that I was locked up with by the name of Seed who is from Barry Farms, which is connected to The Nut. Seed used to treat Killa Reds like a son when we were in FCI Cumberland. I remembered when Seed had told me that Killa Reds was a fuck boy and that he just used him for what he's worth—"COMMISSARY!" he said. He let me know that Killa Reds wasn't originally from The Nut, but that he came through sometimes with a friend of Seed's. I know that Seed can give me the whole scoop on Killa Reds' whereabouts. The disturbing part about the entire situation was how in four hells he happened to coincidentally pull up on me like that. Was it not a coincidence? I mean, he ain't holler at nobody in the complex. He just pulled in, stunted on me and then rolled out. He must've followed me or saw me when I first pulled up. Whatever it was, I had to do my homework on slim.

"Where the hell is this nigga at?" I mumbled to myself, scrolling through my contact list to Big Mike's name and touching the TALK icon.

"What's up lil' bruh, my bad." Big Mike said on the other end of the line as soon as he answered.

"Nigga where you at?" I said to Big Mike.

"I'm coming down Pennsylvania Avenue as we speak. It was major traffic on 495." Big Mike said.

"Oh yea, I forgot you live out VA in west bubbafuck. How far are you now?"

"About five more minutes."

"Aight then, table on you and the first two rounds of Patron."

"That's a bet, I'ma throw in some buffalo wings too, to show my hospility." Big Mike said as he chuckled.

"It's hospitality, fool, and I'm here." I said before ending the call. I scrolled through my music library, feeling like Big Mike as 'Hail Mary' played through my trucks speakers. If werewolves were attacking me, Big Mike would've been my hero because three minutes later, he came flying through the parking lot in his Audi, looking like a silver bullet. Big Mike parked about three spaces down from where I was, in his and Dark China's reserved parking space, before walking over to my truck carrying a black waist pouch. I also noticed that he had a big hole on the bottom right side of his red AKOO shirt. Big Mike opened my passenger side door, sticking just his head inside.

"I'ma run in here and change my clothes real quick." He said as he placed the pouch onto the passenger seat.

"Yea you need to 'cause you running around here on your poo-putt shit, tighten up!" I said. I then grabbed the black pouch before pointing to the hole in Big Mike's shirt. Big Mike then took a step back to look down at his shirt before smiling.

"Oh yea, that fucking mutt bit my damn shirt. Sonya's dumb ass dog kept jumping on me and shit!" Big Mike said.

"Well grab the bag in the backseat, that big brown Shoppers Food Warehouse bag." I said.

Big Mike then shut the passenger side door and opened the rear side passenger door, to retrieve the brown bag from the backseat. Without saying another word, he cradled the bag in his arm like he was holding a baby, closed the rear side door and walked into his building. Ten minutes later, Big Mike was walking out of the building entrance toward my truck dressed in all white everything. Shirt, shorts, cap and shoes with no socks were all white, courtesy of Ralph Lauren POLO. When Big Mike opened my front passenger side door and climbed in, the Chris Tucker "Smokey" from Friday voice came out of me. "Daaaayuum!" I said, as we both burst into laughter.

"Aight, aight, aight nigga. Pull off so I can go bust your ass on this table." Big Mike said. I shifted the car into "drive" and we were on our way to shoot pool at the Galaxy. It took about forty minutes to get to downtown Silver Spring, in Maryland. I was cruising through the parking garage, searching for a parking space when my phone rang.

"Hey mama." I said to my mother.

"Baby, where you at?" My mom asked with a worrisome tone in her voice.

"I'm in Silver Spring, why, what's up?" I replied.

"Well how fast can you get to me?" My mom asked.

"Well ma, it depends on how important it is."

"Louis, I just off the phone with Sharon." My mom said. Sharon is my cousin, Vell's soon to be wife. Sharon is his ride or die chick. She and Vell planned to marry next month, as well as move into the new home that Vell was having built to start themselves a family. Sharon was a beautiful, 37 year old dentist and although at the time she and Vell didn't officially live together, they had full access to each other's homes after they got engaged to keep the trust. Neither had anything to hide from the other. Vell was deeply in love with Sharon, which he always showed.

"And what's up with Sharon, ma, she aight?" I asked my mother as I sat in the middle of the parking garage with my foot on the brake.

"Yea baby, it's not her, it's Vell!" My mother exclaimed, taking a deep breath and letting out a long exhale. "Baby, Sharon found your cousin inside of his home, dead!" My mom said, unable to hold her cry in any longer. The energy from my mom's cry shot straight through my body, like electricity.

"WHAT!" I yelled into the phone, confused and unsure of what I had just heard my mother say. I shifted my truck into park as I listened to my mom talk through her cries about how Sharon found Vell, lying face down inside of his kitchen with bullet holes in the back of his head and upper back area. My mom told me that I could just meet her at Vell's house. We conversed for another four or five minutes, mainly all of them spent trying to calm her down, before I hung up the phone and relayed to Big Mike the situation at hand. Big Mike's facial expression conveyed anger, as well as sadness at the same time. He encouraged me to go to Vell's house to console my family in this time of need and like a true friend, he rode along.

CHAPTER 20

In twenty minutes flat, I was at my cousin Vell's house. The entire ride there was silent. All that was on my mind was how much I wished that it was dream and Killa Reds. Regardless of whether he was involved with this or not, he was a dead man. I planned to kill him just because. When I pulled up to Vell's complex, the police had his parking lot blocked off. No cars in, no cars out.

I parked on the corners of 18th and Montana Avenue. Big Mike told me to go and see what was up with my family, while he sat inside of the truck and talked on the phone to his wife, Sonya. I called my mom's phone to see where she was. She answered and let me know that she had just got out of the cab and was walking toward the police detective to get an update.

After confirming her location in my sight, I disconnected our call and walked across the street to Vell's parking lot. I then leaned back on someone else's fence while from a distance I watched my mom as she conversed with the detective in front of Vell's front yard.

"Young man." A voice called out. I turned around to look behind me and saw an old lady with a hunchback standing inside her doorway.

"Oh, I'm sorry, ma'am." I said, as I stood upwards from her fence and took a step away from her property.

"No, baby, are you okay? Is you some kind of kin folk to the young man that was living over there?" The old lady asked nicely as I turned my whole body to face her.

"Yes, ma'am, that was my first cousin." I respectfully replied.

"Well he was a nice young man and I liked him, but I don't like them pigs." The old lady said, pointing towards a police car which made me chuckle.

"Yes ma'am, me neither." I replied.

"Looks here young man, I want you to turn around with your backside facing me, okay?" The old lady said. She waved her hand, signaling for me to turn my body. I then turned around and leaned back on her fence. "You didn't hear this come outta my mouth, ya hear me?" The old lady asked as I nodded my head up and down in confirmation. "It was a dark colored car with the dark windows, that I saw drive out of this parking lot a couple of hours ago. When I heard a car door slam, it made me look out of the window. That's when I saw that car speeding off, making that screeching noise with its tires. I thought nothing of it, just figured they were in a rush, but I did have that ol' feeling like something wasn't right a little while later. After about thirty minutes, maybe, I heard screaming and yelling from that pretty little girl that be's coming over here all the time." The old lady said, as my mom looked in my direction to locate me before she began to walk away from the police detective toward me. "'Help! Help!' is what she said." The old lady finished, before I heard her front door close.

"Get off them peoples' fence, boy!" My mother yelled while walking toward me. I stood up from the fence before glancing behind me, seeing not a soul. I walked toward my mother and greeted her with a tight hug and kiss on her cheek.

"What they say?" I asked my mother, still hugging her in my arms.

"No motive, no suspects at the time. They still have Sharon, over there questioning her. I'ma probably just wait on her and I'll ride back with her to keep her company." My mother said as she peeled away from my grasp to look into my eyes. "Louis, I don't know what you still be doing out there in those streets but I just pray that it stops. I do not want to have to bury you. You and Vell are supposed to bury me. Now both of my nephews are dead. I love you, son. I just want you to fly straight, son, please. For me." My mother pled as I stood there in silence for a few seconds, daydreaming.

I then snapped out of my trance and kissed my mom on her forehead before telling her that I love her. "I'ma call you later, momma." I said to my mother before walking back to my truck and climbing into the driver seat.

"You aight, bruh?" Big Mike asked.

"Yea, I'm cool, I'll be better soon." I said as I scrolled through my phone to Seed's number. Just three rings later,

"Hello?" Seed said on the other line.

"Seed, what's up bruh?" I said.

"Ain't shit, who this?"

"This Lou, from The Cruddy."

"Who?"

"Lou, nigga!"

"Cruddy Island Lou?"

"Yea, nigga. I just said that."

"Well goddamn, stranger, you must be in trouble or some'n, calling me?" Seed said, laughing at his own comment.

"Naw, my nigga, I'm tryna get the 4-1-1 on your boy Reds." I said.

"Reds? Who the hell is Reds?"

"The fuck boy Killa Reds that was in Cumberland."

"Oh yea, slim that be hood hopping."

"Yea, him." I confirmed.

"Okay, okay. I'm with you now. Well all I know is that he be hustling out Oxon Hill in Maryland, around some hood called River View Terrace but he live over there by Montana, on 18th Street in Northeast somewhere." While seed was talking, I then turned around in my seat to look back at the street sign and thought to myself, 'I'm on 18th Street, now.' I continued to listen to Seed talk.

"You probably wanna swing out Maryland and catch him out there if it's that important. I saw him on the Southside once pushing a smacked out, all black Camaro joint. It was like a 2011 or 2012 joint, too." Seed said as I nodded my head up and down.

"Thanks, bruh, I appreciate 'cha." I said to Seed.

"Yezzir! And do your homework slim, trace your tracks aight." Seed said.

"For sure, bruh." I replied.

"And next time you call me, it better be to just chill and not 'cause you want some'n." Seed said as we both laughed.

"You right, slim. I'ma hit you this week." I said before hanging up our call.

"Found what you looking for?" Big Mike asked me, as he texted in his phone.

"I hope so. You going back to your car?" I asked Big Mike as I shifted my gear into drive, awaiting a response.

"Yea." Big Mike said as I pulled off. "Nah! I mean no bruh, I'ma go around W Street." Big Mike suddenly said, changing his mind.

"W Street?" I asked.

"Yea, my lil' peoples Nook live around the 'toga. I'ma chill with him and have him drop me off later." Big Mike said, as he pointed up Montana Avenue. The 'toga was short for a neighborhood housing project called Saratoga which was literally around the corner from Vell's house. Sixty seconds tops, I then pulled over on the corner of Brentwood Road and W Street, to let Big Mike out. After he stepped out of the car I immediately drove back around the corner to 18th Street to see if I could spot Killa Reds' car. After a minor search...bingo! His car was parked in front of a greenish looking house on 18th Street. I spent a few seconds observing his car before pulling off in pursuit to Cruddy Island to execute my plan. The clock on my truck dashboard read 9:22 PM so I wasn't working with too much time. I had to act fast if I planned to succeed.

CHAPTER 21

I pulled in a parking lot in Paradise that was attached to a basketball court and found a parking space by a dumpster can. I hopped out of my truck and raced through the breezeway into Faith Court. After walking inside of Wee-Wees house, I ordered her to come talk to me inside the back room. She immediately followed me to my stash room. "What's up, nephew?" Wee-Wee asked in concern.

"Aye, you think one of your buddies are tryna rent out their whip?" I asked.

"Snoop crazy ass just left outta here and went up the street to grab some'n from up Mayfair for us. He just left out, so you could probably catch him." Wee-Wee said as she stepped aside, allowing me to rush past her. I jetted out the building and ran through another breezeway that was connected to another parking lot directly on the opposite side of where I was parked in Faith Court. As soon as I walked out of the breezeway, I saw Snoop, standing at Mr. Charles' ice cream truck talking to Tre Pound, Lil Chris and Q-Tip.

"Aye, Snoop!" I yelled while walking toward him, making him turn around to look and see who was calling his name.

"Hey, neph! Owww!" Snoop yelled, as he walked toward me jokingly, in his George Jefferson walk.

"Come holler at me." I said while chuckling. One thing about Snoop, his black bald headed ass would make you laugh and smile during the worst times.

"Whatcha need, nephew? I ain't do it!" Snoop shouted, making me laugh a little harder.

"Naw, unc. Let me holler at you real quick." I said as I placed my arm around his shoulder and lowered my voice. "Look, I'ma need your wheels real quick. I got $50 dollars for you." I said as I pulled my money out of my pocket.

"For $50 dollars you can have the damn car!" Owww!" Snoop said, making me laugh while I peeled a fifty dollar bill from the wad of cash I held in my hand. "Sike! Ma-ma would kill your uncle Snoop if I sold her car, you know that's ma-ma car nephew."

"She don't know I got it." Snoop said as he grabbed the fifty dollar bill out my hand before handing me the car keys. "I parked down there to the right, neph." Snoop said, pointing to a fleet of cars that was in the parking lot. "It's the Oldsmobile station wagon, nephew." Snoop said. I started walking through the parking lot to locate the station wagon. After I spotted the car, I fast walked back to Wee-Wee's house to grab my pistols. I grabbed my chrome .45 Taurus, and my big dumb ass .40 caliber highpoint. I know what they say about highpoints and how they are some bullshit guns in which I agree, but they do kill.

I didn't plan to go to war with a highpoint. Highpoints are good throw away guns. I brought the Taurus along just in case I had more action than expected. Better safe than sorry. After making sure my weapons were fully loaded with Hydra-Shok bullets, I cocked them both, placing one in the head, before zipping them both into a backpack that I had stored inside of the room. I then made my way out of the apartment, into the station wagon, on my way to see my victim. It took between ten to fifteen minutes for me to get to Killa Reds house in this slow ass car. I found me a parking spot on the same side of the street under a tree about four vehicle links behind his car. I was parked directly behind a black Ford Excursion that camouflaged me from distant eyesight.

After I cut off the engine, I glanced at my black G-Shock watch which read 10:16 PM. It was still pretty early, and I saw a group of three young teenaged boys between the ages of sixteen and nineteen walk past on the sidewalk. Neither of them attempted to look over to their right to see me.

The street was pretty dark, and being that I parked behind the Excursion and under the tree, it blocked any light from entering and made my location look darker and me unnoticeable. There was no noise or movement on the street for the next hour until I heard a house door shut close and heard someone laughing up ahead.

I immediately adjusted and sat up in my seat and slightly leaned to my right into the passenger seat to see if I saw anyone.

I then heard a gate screech as it opened to see what looked to be Killa Reds walking out of the yard before pressing the unlock button on his hand held keypad. The rear lights of his Camaro flashed as I heard the locks to his car doors unlock. He opened the passenger side door of his car as I retrieved the .40 caliber highpoint out of the book bag quickly.

I zipped the book bag close before quietly climbing out of the station wagon with the backpack strapped over my shoulder. I softly closed the car door enough to make the interior lights go out. I then crept from behind the Excursion on the driver side and saw that Killa Reds was sitting inside of the passenger seat of his car, on the curb, searching through a small pile of papers inside of his glove compartment. I then crept from the street, around the rear of his car to the passenger side where he was. Before Killa Reds could even look up to realize what was happening, I already had the .40 caliber pointing two feet from his head. "Shhh!" is what I said as Killa Reds simultaneously looked upwards while hopping backwards into his seat with his mouth wide open in awe and his eyes as big as a horse's.

"Don't say shit." I whispered. "Just climb over in the driver's seat before I put your brains in 'em. I ain't gonna kill your dumb ass if you cooperate." I lied to Killa Reds in order to get him to cooperate silently.

"Okay, o-kay." Killa Reds said as he climbed over the middle console to the drivers' seat.

I then quietly sat inside the passenger seat before closing the door as well as the glove compartment to kill the lights.

"Start it up and pull off." I demanded. He immediately cooperated

without saying a word.

When he started his car, the music that played through his speakers

was a song called, 'Straight From Da Mud' by a rapper named Dee

Boog. With the knuckles of my left index finger and middle finger, I

turned down the music just enough for him to clearly hear me talk.

"First, put on your seatbelt, then go to New York Avenue and make

a right going towards Florida Avenue. I want you to pull inside the

Tyler House parking lot, by the swimming pool." I demanded to Killa

Reds, as I leaned my right shoulder onto the passenger door with the

.40 caliber in my right hand pointed directly at Killa Reds' body.

With no hesitation, he did as demanded. I held the pistol low by my

stomach, just in case he was tempted to play super hero. I had him

place his seatbelt on for two reasons. One, so we would not get pulled

over by police unnecessarily, and two, so he wouldn't be able to jump

out of the car without being shot up. I could see his mind wandering

in deep thought from his facial expressions, but he knew better than

to try something stupid that would risk his life.

"Anything extra, and I promise you gonna die as well as me, from a shoot-out with the cops. Cooperate properly, and you will live Reds, I promise you." I said in a calming tone. Killa Reds pulled into a parking space behind the Tyler House swimming pool. Killa Reds shut off the engine, as instructed.

"Come on, Lou. We can dead this shit, bruh. This shit ain't that serious." Killa Reds pled.

"Ha-haaa, muthafucka!" I spat back at him in a deranged tone. "You think I'ma fool, huh? You think I'm sweet or some'n, huh?"

"Naw, bruh, what you talking 'bout?" he plead.

"You tryna rock me to sleep like you did my cousin, huh?"

"WHAT!"

"What, shit, nigga! I'm hipped to you!" I angrily said to Killa Reds, clenching my teeth.

"Hipped to what?" Killa Reds asked.

"Man fuck all the dumb shit." I said, adjusting my backpack and placing it on my lap as I unzipped the zipper.

"Man that shit from earlier was about nothin', bruh. The only reason I pulled up on you was because of a note that was left in my windshield wiper earlier. I said to myself 'let me check this out', so I circled around Montana, and saw you get out of your truck and walk into that house. I pulled over and parked outside of the parking lot and waited for you to come out. I told my lil' man Ray-Ray who was in the car with me that I was about to fuck with you real quick. I took this shit as a game, bruh, nothing serious." Killa Reds pled. He then pointed to his glove compartment. "Look in there, it's a yellow piece of paper. That's what I was looking for earlier before you kidnapped a nigga. I was 'bout to show my peoples." Killa Reds said. I opened the glove compartment, rumbling through paper before I saw a folded yellow piece.

After grabbing the yellow piece of paper, I closed the glove compartment. I unfolded the piece of paper and held it with my left hand, my right hand still clutching the .40 cal, pointing it toward Killa Reds as I read the note:

YOU WANT LOU?

HE'LL BE IN MONTANA AT 6 O'CLOCK.

LOOK FOR A GRAY KIA TRUCK.

FROM A FRIEND OF A FRIEND.

The note definitely struck a nerve. As I sat thinking about how and who, Killa Reds interrupted my train of thought.

"Told you, my nigga! I ain't tryna get at you, but somebody definitely wants me to." He said.

"Yea... you right." I said, nodding my head up and down.

BLOCKA! BLOCKA!

The two shots hit Killa Reds on the right side of his chest and on his neck, directly under his right jaw bone. He curled up his upper body, trying to apply pressure to the bullet wound to his neck, as blood gushed out.

"But you can't." I said to Killa Reds before I placed the .40 caliber to the back of his head, directly behind his ear.

BLOCKA!

Killa Reds' head collapsed onto his door panel as his entire body went limp and his blood splattered and leaked down the driver side window. In a hurry, I placed the .40 caliber Highpoint inside of the backpack and stuffed the note into my jeans pocket. With my shirt tail, I began wiping down everything I assumed I touched. Keeping my head low to avoid my face being seen by any inconspicuous cameras, I walked quickly but calmly out of the parking lot, zipping my backpack closed before hoisting it onto my back.

I cut over to First Street, and took that route down to New Jersey Avenue to my apartment building. I crept inside of the apartment, trying not to wake Tanya from her slumber. I immediately emptied my pockets, took off all of my clothes and stuffed them inside of the backpack and placed it into Little Bo's bedroom closet. I then took a shower. I did understand that if Tanya woke up that it would seem as if I was attempting to wash the scent of another woman off of me but at that point I didn't really care what Tanya would think. After showering, I wrapped my towel around my waist before walking into my bedroom and putting on a pair of boxer briefs. I walked over to the bed, sat down on the edge and started thinking about that note, which reminded me to shred it and flush it down the toilet. I walked back into my room and stretched out in the bed next to Tanya, analyzing my life.

CHAPTER 22

The next morning when I awoke, Tanya was dressed and ready to go to church service with my mom and Sharon, like they do every Sunday. When I looked at the clock on the nightstand, it read 7:07 AM. That let me know that they were planning to attend the 8 o'clock service. I rolled over in the bed as Tanya was walking back into the room.

"You 'bout to go get mom dukes?" I asked Tanya.

"Duuuhh. You figured that out all by yourself, Einstein?" She replied sarcastically, chuckling at her own comment.

"Well, drop me off around the way to get my truck then, smart ass." I said jokingly from the bed.

"Well you better hurry up and come on." Tanya exclaimed, as she walked back into the living room.

It took me no more than 10 minutes to brush my teeth, wash my face and throw some of my clothes on. I then grabbed the backpack from out of Little Bo's room and slid my cell phone into my front jeans pocket. "Come on, T, I'm ready!" I shouted to Tanya. She then stood up from our living room sofa, looking me and my outfit up and down before bursting into laughter as she grabbed the car keys from the living room table. She then walked out of the front door as I followed. When we got around my hood, Tanya parked into a parking space inside of my mother's building parking lot before she pulled her cell phone out of her purse to call my mom to let her know that she was outside waiting. I kissed Tanya on her cheek before grabbing my backpack and climbing out of the car.

I walked directly around the corner to where my truck was parked. I climbed inside of my truck, placed the backpack into the front passenger seat and pulled my cell phone out of my pocket. I had three missed calls and three unheard voicemail messages. I went directly to the voice messages, hearing that the first one was from Little Bo.

"Daddy, call me when you can. Kevin Durant and John Wall were here yesterday. Call me dad, love you." Little Bo said excitedly. The next message was from my mom.

"Hello, my son. You make sure you call me and come over to talk to me later after church sometime. I know you probably knocked out sleep. This is very important son, love ya." My mom said.

"I'm calling you before you get to church anyway." I mumbled to myself before the last voice message played.

"Aye, slim. This Seed. That damn beehive you talked to me about yesterday is gone. Someone must've knocked it down last night, breaking news slim. Oh yea, just to let you know, Lump called me last night and said that your man Big Mizzike, called him a few days ago and asked him about the exact same info you needed. I guess he had a bee problem, too. He must've stolen your honey, slim. Hit my phone later when you get up, slim." Seed finished, as I sat there in my truck for a few minutes in deep thought. After dismissing thoughts about Big Mike trying to set me up, my phone lit up with an incoming call. I looked at the screen and saw that it was my mother. I pressed the volume button to turn on my ringer sound before answering.

"Hello, mother." I said, in a soft and sweet tone of voice.

"Hello, son." My mother replied with a disappointing tone in her voice. "You come to my domain without saying a word to me, my son?"

"Yes ma'am, I apologize momma, but I had to make a run real quick." I replied.

"And that run was more important than me?"

"No, ma, and you know that."

"I know, I just wanna hear you say it." My mom said, as she chuckled over the phone. "Did you get my message?" She asked.

"Yes, I did. I just heard it a couple of minutes ago." I replied.

"Okay, well you make sure to call me immediately after our 8 o'clock service. We should be done around ten." My mom said.

"I'll call you at eleven, then, so that I can come and holla at you."

"Okay, I should be in the house by then. We stop at Langston Golf Course on Benning Road every Sunday to get some breakfast. You let me know if you want something and I'll grab it for ya."

"Naw, ma, I'm good. I'ma make sure I'm en route by eleven o'clock, okay?"

"Okay baby."

"Love you, momma."

"I love you too, baby." My mother said, before ending our call.

I then started up my truck and headed out of the parking lot. Seconds later, I was pulling into another parking lot in Mayfair. While cruising through the parking lot, I saw X-Man walking out of a back door of one of the buildings. I tapped on my horn to get his attention. As I backed into a parking space, X-Man walked toward my truck, opening the door to climb inside as soon as I was parked. I removed the backpack from the passenger seat and moved it to my lap as he climbed in.

"What's up, Lou?" X-Man asked as we fist bumped.

"Ain't shit." I replied. "Aye, I need a favor lil' bruh." I said.

"What's up, what you need?" X-Man asked.

"I need you to get rid of this jimmy jam for me. I'ma give you a hundred, and you can keep whatever you sell it for." I said.

"Aight, I got you. I thought you was gonna ask me some'n complicated." X-Man joked, chuckling. I removed the .40 caliber Highpoint pistol from out of the backpack, along with the .45 Taurus handgun.

"Hold down this Taurus for me, but make this bullshit ass Highpoint vanish ASAP, but not around here, feel me?" I said before handing him both pistols and then dug into my pants pocket and counted out five twenty dollar bills. X-Man stuffed the money into his own pants pocket before placing both handguns into the waistline of his jeans.

"I got you, bruh." X-Man assured me while climbing out of my truck. He then walked back through the back door of the building he had come out of.

I got out of my truck with the backpack in hand and emptied the clothing that was inside into the large green dumpster garbage can that sat at the end of the parking lot. As soon as I climbed back into my truck, my cell phone rang. The caller ID displayed an unknown number that read 202-555-6155. I answered the call. "Hello, who this?"

"This me, nephew, Wee-Wee." Wee-Wee said from the other end of the line.

"Oh, what's up, auntie!" I replied.

"Where you at? Snoop need his car—this his phone I'm calling you from right here."

"Tell him to walk out to the street now, I'm coming around the circle as we speak. Tell him to meet me at the bus stop by your court right now, auntie."

"Okay baby, he's leaving out now."

"Aight, cool." I hung up the phone then proceeded to pull out of the parking lot and sped around the ONE-WAY street to see Uncle Snoop standing at the bus stop. I pulled up, stopping directly in front of the bus stop before Snoop climbed in.

"Lou, Ma-Ma gonna kill me, neph." Snoop said.

"Why you say that, Snoop?" I asked.

"'Cause this ain't her car, owwww!" Snoop said, triggering me to laugh before I turned up the volume of the music that played through my speakers. It was Top Dolla Sweizy's old radio single, "High Five To The Plug". Snoop bounced up and down, bopping his head to the music that WPGC 95.5 played for the next fifteen minutes, until we pulled up directly across the street from where his Oldsmobile station wagon was parked. "That's Ma-Ma car right there!" Snoop yelled excitedly as I dug into my pants pocket and handed him his car keys along with another $50 dollar bill, for his convenience. When Snoop got out of my truck, I waited until he started his engine before pulling off. In my rearview, I saw Snoop pulling out of the parking spot, which gave me relief.

CHAPTER 23

I made a right turn onto New York Avenue from Montana Avenue. It took me no time to get to my house due to the lack of traffic on Sunday mornings. If it were a Sunday evening before or after a Redskins game, then I would have still been on back streets ducking traffic.

As soon as I got into my house, I returned Little Bo's call. He had sounded so excited on my voicemail earlier. "Hey old man." Little Bo said when he picked up the phone.

"What's up, lil' homie, you aight?" I asked Little Bo in an excited tone of voice and a smile big enough to assume I won the lottery. Little Bo always made me smile every time I saw him or heard his voice.

He was my heart and I made sure that it was no secret.

"Dad, you must be getting older every time I leave home." Little Bo said dramatically.

"Why you say that lil' homie?"

"Because, you even starting to move slow to call me back." Little Bo joked, making me burst into laughter.

"That was a good one, Bo." I said into the phone.

"Hey dad! I took pictures with Kevin Durant and John Wall."

"Oh yea?! So you saying K.D. and John Wall were lucky enough to take a picture with you?" I corrected Little Bo.

"Yea, well I guess so." Little Bo agreed. "Hey dad, I have to get ready for drills. I was doing stretches before you called, so I'ma try to call you back later when I'm available, okay." Little Bo said.

"Okay, sir, you can give me a call whenever your schedule is clear, Mr. Bo." I said, chuckling into the phone.

"Okay, old man. Love you, Pops, talk to you later. Gotta go." Little Bo said, rushing me off the phone.

"I love you too, Bo." I said before Little Bo hung up. I was feeling pretty hungry so I went to the kitchen and pulled some turkey bacon, a carton of eggs and a pack of cheese from out of the refrigerator. I then grabbed the Aunt Jemima pancake mix from the cabinet above the stove that stored the canned goods.

Afterwards, I walked into my bedroom and stripped down to my socks and boxer briefs. Next, I laid out the clothes that I had planned to wear for the day onto the bed before going back to the kitchen, cooking breakfast and eating. I then washed my dishes before washing my ass.

I stood in the shower for at least thirty minutes, enjoying the therapy of the hot water pressure hitting my body. Meditating about this past week, I thought back to when I first met **Big Mike**. My mind thought about everything. From the halfway house, to the statement that Killa Reds made last night before I took his life. Nothing was making sense.

Why would Big Mike want me gone? After dismissing the thought and settling with the assumption that Killa Reds was trying to turn me against Big Mike, I finally got out of the shower and prepared myself for my day. I got myself dressed and ready to go before glancing at the kitchen clock which read 9:54 AM. 'Momma's almost done with church service,' I thought to myself before leaving the house in pursuit of Cruddy Island. I pulled in Mayfair's first parking lot on the Hayes Street side, and parked. I sat in the parking lot for almost thirty minutes, listening to 2Pac's 'All Eyez On Me' album, before I decided to call my mother and check her location.

I was curious to see what she wanted to talk to me about. My dashboard clock read 10:42 AM. "Hey Louis." My mother answered the phone after one ring.

"Hey momma, where you at?" I asked.

"We're pulling down Hayes Street now, about to arrive at my Kingdom soon. Where are you?"

"I'm about to be there, also, mother." I said.

"Well get off my phone." My mother said sarcastically, hanging up the phone on me. I threw my truck into drive, and seconds later I was pulling into Unity Court. As I parked, I saw Tanya and my mother walking into her building. I hurried out of my truck and rushed into the building behind them.

After I locked my mom's front door, I turned around and saw Tanya standing inside of the kitchen, staring at me with a porn star seduction look in her eyes before licking her tongue at me. My mom then walked into the living room, coming from her bedroom. I burst out laughing at how fast Tanya straightened her fuck face when my mom came into eyesight.

"What's so funny, mister?" My mom asked, as she walked over to me and kissed me on my cheek.

"Nothing, ma."

"Ain't no inside jokes in my house. Now come back here and let me talk to you for a sec." My mother said, leading me to the back room. I glanced over at Tanya while following my mother, and she put up her middle finger at me as soon as we got out of my moms' eyesight. Once inside the room I flopped back on my moms' bed as she closed the room door. She then sat in her rocking chair which sat in the far corner of her bedroom on the opposite side of her bed by a window. I sat up straight on the edge of her bed, giving my mom my undivided attention as she took a deep breath before exhaling.

"Louis, Louis, Louis..." my mother said, shaking her head from left to right. "Sharon is going through it. I had a long conversation with her last night. You know she spent the night over here.

About an hour after we were talking, the lead detective called her phone and asked her if she had saw anyone leave or anyone that was standing around the house when she arrived with a red shirt. Vell's fence caught a piece of red fabric on it. The detective said that he was going to take it to their lab and do DNA testing on it." My mom said as my mind wandered in deep thought. "Are you with me, son?"

"Yea, I'm with you ma, go ahead." I replied, snapping out of my daydream as my mother continued,

"Sharon said something about Darnell. She said that Da'Vell had mentioned something to her about the boy named Germaine, and how he was supposed to be getting released soon. Did he mention anything like that to you?" My mother asked.

"Naw, he ain't say nothing about that to me." I replied while collecting my thoughts. "Aye, ma, do your computer in the other room still work?" I asked.

"Yea, boy." She nodded in acknowledgement. "I don't do nothing but play solitaire on there. I don't ever use that internet thing. I be paying for it for no reason."

"No you don't, ma." I replied, standing up from my mother's bed before zooming out of her bedroom into my old bedroom, which was now set up as an office. I walked in and closed the room door behind me for some privacy.

I sat at the computer desk and shook the mouse to cancel the screen saver. I then double clicked the Netscape Navigator icon on the home screen, which opened up the webpage Google.com. Inside of the search bar I typed, "Darnell Sanchez, Murder, Washington D.C., 1996" and pressed ENTER on the keyboard. In less than two seconds, I found a small brief paragraph with a link under it that read, "HOMICIDEWATCH.COM". I double clicked the link which opened up another page with exactly what I was searching for—my cousin D-Bo's murder case.

HOMICIDE SUSPECT, MICHAEL GERMAINE MITCHELL, WAS SENTENCED TO 20 YEARS TO LIFE IN PRISON AS PART OF A PLEA AGREEMENT, FOR THE MURDER OF DARNELL SANCHEZ ON JULY 18TH 1996, AT APPROXIMATELY 8:00 PM IN THE 3500 BLOCK OF JAY STREET IN NORTHEAST, D.C. DUE TO A PLEA AGREEMENT, MR. MITCHELL WOULD NOT BE SENTENCED TO A MANDATORY LIFE SENTENCE AS HE WOULD HAD HE BEEN FOUND GUILTY IN TRIAL. MITCHELL WILL BE ELIGIBLE FOR PAROLE IN 2016.

I sat there staring into a blank space, replaying my entire relationship

with Big Mike. From the first day that we met up until the last time

that I saw him yesterday. Tears begun to form in my eyes, angry

because of the betrayal, but more so because I felt like I had played a

part in the death of my cousin, Vell. In a matter of seconds, I fell into

a deep daydream of when I was a child watching the Forrest Gump

movie. "Life is like a box of chocolates. Ya' never know what 'cha

gonna get." is what Forrest said from the television.

"LOUIS!" My mother interrupted, snapping me out of the trance before I looked towards the doorway. My mother stood there placing her hand over her mouth the same way that she did when D-Bo was murdered, shocked at the state of mind she saw me, her only child, in. She walked over to me and hugged me around my shoulders before kissing me on my forehead. She then leaned down toward my ear and whispered, "Think, my son. If not for me, for Little Bo. If not for Little Bo, then for Tanya. If not for Tanya, then do it for yourself. Just take your time and think. I love you, son." My mother pled before once again kissing me on my forehead and walking out of the room, closing the door. For the next hour or so, I sat there and thought.

I thought about my past and thought about my future. I thought about my family, my friends and my enemies. The more thinking that I did, the more that I came to realize that with every action, the answer to it is just a simple thought.

CHAPTER 24

When I left my mother's house, I drove straight home to relax my mind. I did a hell of a lot of thinking. It seems as if every time you're putting a plan together, something always tries to distract you. Like my phone ringing. It was Big Mike.

I answered and listened to Big Mike talk excitedly about how great of a day he had and how he wanted to meet up with me the following day to re-up. I agreed to meet him at 1700 hours at the Groom Spot. He asked about my well-being, and how I had been holding up after Vell's death. I confirmed that I was okay and handling it well.

I played the entire situation cool, not showing any emotional signs of anger toward Big Mike. I didn't want to show any signs that I was hipped to Big Mike. A wise man can act dumb but a dummy cannot act wise.

At one point during our conversation, I laughed at practically nothing to show good humor and to keep Big Mike comfortable. After we ended our phone conversation, I thought about a book that my partner Kalvin had turned me onto. It was titled, 'The Secret' by Rhonda Byrne. It speaks about the power of the mind and how you can think things into existence. That's when I knew that my plan was meant to be so I decided to speed up the process. The next morning, I had to make a few calls. The first was to Enterprise Car Rental. They told me to come and pick up the 2017 Ford Mustang that I rented for two days at noon. Next, I called my Dominican partner, Pierre.

I met Pierre in the feds and we kept a mutual relationship ever since. We don't see each other much, except on Instagram, but we do call and check up on each other at least twice a week. He told me to meet him at four that afternoon, in the parking lot of Prince George's Plaza Shopping Mall in Hyattsville, Maryland.

Lastly, I called Big Mike, to make sure that he wasn't drunk talking when he called last night. After he confirmed that everything was a go, I then started phase two of the five P's, "PREPARATION!" It was time to start my day.

I saw Cold Billy, Light Skinned Domo and Fahmi standing in the parking lot of the corner store, conversing. I grew up with all three of these good men, so I had more trust and respect level for them, then I would for someone I met in, let's say, the feds. Cold Billy and Fahmi, chose the smart route in life. Even though they both had their minor run-ins with the law, they rose from the aftermath against all odds. They both became successful businessmen and ran successful non-profit organizations as well. Light Skinned Domo, on the other hand, chose the streets. After serving a short prison term, Domo was finally finding success in his passion, strippers. He opened up a strip club out Fort Washington, Maryland, which I hadn't been to yet but I planned to go and show my support really soon. I drove into the parking lot and parked beside a black 760 BMW that they were standing next to.

Leaving my truck engine running, I climbed out and shook their hands before asking if either of them could drop me off up the street at the car rental place on Benning Road. Fahmi said, "No problem," since we were closest to his car, the 760 BMW. Cold Billy and Domo decided to tag along for the ride. After I parked my truck behind the corner store on Kenilworth Terrace, I climbed into Fahmi's car, and about three minutes later, I was getting out in front of Enterprise Car Rental.

I went inside and went through the proper procedures before being handed the keys to a black Ford Mustang. I then drove directly back around my hood and chilled in Cruddy Island with my homies Kenric, Buck and Drew, reminiscing about old times in the hood until about three thirty that afternoon. I then made my way to meet up with Pierre.

I circled through the mall parking lot for a couple of minutes before Pierre called my phone, informing me that he was parked in a green Tahoe on the backside of the mall in front of the Ross department store.

I urgently found his location and backed into a parking space next to the passenger side of his truck. Leaving the Mustang engine running, I climbed into the passenger seat of Pierre's truck.

After embracing each other with dap, we small talked for several minutes, mainly about how we needed to hang out more often. Pierre then handed me a small brown paper bag before I handed him a sandwich bag full of cash.

"Is this the way you're going now papi?" Pierre asked out of concern.

"Naw, P, this here is for a friend of mine, you know how I live." I replied, before fist bumping Pierre's hand as I climbed out of his truck and back into the driver seat of the Mustang. We tapped our horns at each other as we drove our separate ways. When I pulled into the parking lot behind Wee-Wee's apartment, brown paper bag in hand, it was 4:33 PM.

When I walked inside, Wee-Wee was sitting in the living room watching re-runs of Martin, looking bored as hell before I rushed into the back room to finish executing my plan. I opened the room closet and grabbed my five shot .38 snub nose revolver, affectionately named Ms. Palmer from how it just hid in the palm of my hand.

I loved it so much because it had no visible hammer like most revolvers. I bought Ms. Palmer back in 2007 from a friend of a friend when I was at NC A&T Homecoming Celebration in Greensboro, North Carolina for $75 bucks.

I had let off a couple of rounds when I first purchased the gun to make sure that it worked. I never shot it after that because I never had a need to. After making sure Ms. Palmer was loaded with live ammunition, I then wrapped the pistol into a wash rag before tucking it at the small of my back into my belt line.

Next, I grabbed a backpack that I had in the closet and stuffed it with towels and washcloths. I then sat the paper bag that I got from Pierre inside before zipping it closed. I walked into the living room to holler at Wee-Wee. Being that she looked so bored, I figured that I'd give her something to do. I handed Wee-Wee my cellphone, and instructed her to answer it every time that it rang without saying anything.

"Just pick up the call and wait for 60 to 120 seconds, before hanging up the call. Be inconsistent with the time and keep the phone with you at all times." I explained to Wee-Wee before giving her $100 dollars in ones and fives.

I then lied to her and told her that I heard somebody up Mayfair got some '88 crack, but that I didn't know who. I told her to spend a little at a time until she found out who. "Make sure you make a few trips." I said to Wee-Wee. The clock on her wall read 4:55 PM. Perfect timing is everything.

CHAPTER 25

I rushed out of Wee-Wee's apartment and hopped into the Mustang at 4:58 PM. I then pulled out of the parking lot and drove within the speed limit down Kenilworth Avenue.

When I turned onto Frolic Lane, I saw Big Mike's silver Audi parked directly in front of the warehouse's entry way. I parked directly beside Big Mike's car, on the far side of the street's entrance, camouflaging the Mustang from any passerby. See, I'm a firm believer of, "What you don't see, you can't tell."

While I was parking, I looked inside of Big Mike's car to see if I saw anyone or any movement. I saw nothing. After readjusting the .38 revolver in my back for sturdiness, comfort and convenience, I climbed out of the Mustang, backpack in hand, and flicked my shirt tail, making sure the revolver wasn't revealed.

I walked into the abandoned warehouse and followed the sound of the voice that I heard as soon as I walked in. The closer I got, the clearer it became. "Come with me, Hail Mary! Nigga, run, quick, see... what do we have here now?" Big Mike sang as I walked into the large empty and open space, facing Big Mike's backside. As I took a couple of steps into the open area, the wood floor made a creaking sound confirming its age.

Big Mike stopped singing and he swiftly turned his body to look toward my direction. "Goddamn, lil' homie," he exclaimed with a smile on his face like he was happy to see me. "What's up with your phone? I just called you 'bout two minutes ago and that joint just picked up and then hung up." Big Mike explained, making phone gestures with his hand.

"For real?" I said, feigning surprise. "That joint been trippin' a lot lately. I'ma go grab me a new one probably tomorrow or something." I said. I then walked closer to Big Mike and dropped the backpack on the ground about two feet away from him. He dug into the side pocket of his cargo pants, pulled out a wad of cash and handed it to me as I approached him.

"It's all there. Nice doing business with you, bruh." Big Mike said as he winked then continued, "Look here, this shit is moving. I gotta go bust a few moves real quick then I'll be getting right back at you. You aight though?" Big Mike asked while reaching out to dap my hand as he moved past me.

"Yea, I'm cool home team."

"Aight then, just hit my phone if you need me." Big Mike replied, walking toward the entrance I'd came through. I turned to face Big Mike's backside and dug into the small of my back to retrieve the revolver as I stuffed the wad of cash into my back pocket. I removed the wash cloth from Ms. Palmer and pointed the pistol at Big Mike's backside.

"Big homie!" I yelled while slowly taking steps towards Big Mike's direction.

"What's up...what the..." Big Mike exclaimed out of shock as he turned around to reply to my calling. "Lou! What you doing, slim?"

"Damn big homie, I had major plans for us." I said in a disappointed tone. I stopped my approach five feet away from Big Mike.

"Sssss!" Big Mike hissed, before sucking his teeth and chuckling. "You know shawty, you smarter than I thought you to be." Big Mike said, as he dropped the backpack onto the floor beside his foot. "All I wanna know is, what gave me up?" He continued, as he chuckled once again while I shook my head from left to right in shame.

"You have no remorse, huh?" I asked Big Mike before he snapped.

"Why should I?!" He yelled angrily. "Your cousin took my whole damn family from me! Killing D-Bo was business. He brought that on himself, Lou, and Vell knew that!" Big Mike yelled.

"On himself, huh?" I asked sarcastically.

"Yea, on himself!" Big Mike exclaimed. "And as far as Vell... revenge is like the SWEETEST JOY next to getting pussy!" He sang in his 2Pac voice, as saliva flew from his lips.

"And that's probably some of the truest shit you ever said." I replied before POW! POW! POW!

The three shots from the .38 revolver ripped through Big Mike's chest like a core exercise, sending him to his knees with his eyes wide open. He was holding his chest like he was pledging an allegiance.

His body finally collapsed onto its side into a fetal position. At this point my heart was racing my thoughts, as anxiety showed itself through the sweat in my palms.

I took a few steps toward Big Mike and quickly picked up the backpack as I took a step away from Big Mike's arm reach. Unzipping the backpack, I removed the small brown paper bag from inside of it. I opened the paper bag and emptied ten bundles of dope on the floor around Big Mike's body as he laid there gasping for oxygen. I placed the brown bag back inside of the backpack before zipping it closed. I then removed the .38 revolver from my pants pocket and pointed it at Big Mike. He cut his bloody eyes upwards at me and between breaths, blood gushing from his mouth, he smiled and laughed.

POW! POW!

The last two shots hit Big Mike directly in his forehead, ending his suffering.

"The sweetest joy..." I whispered to myself as I exited the abandoned warehouse.

CHAPTER 26 – EPILOGUE

THE UNIDENTIFIED BODY WHICH WAS FOUND LAST NIGHT IN AN ABANDONED WAREHOUSE ON FROLICH LANE IN HYATTSVILLE, MARYLAND HAS BEEN IDENTIFIED AS 40 YEAR OLD MICHAEL GERMAINE MITCHELL. MITCHELL'S BODY, AS WELL AS AN UNTESTED CONTROLLED SUBSTANCE LOCAL AUTHORITIES SAY THEY BELIEVE IT TO BE HEROIN, WAS FOUND BY A PATROL OFFICER OF THE HYATTSVILLE POLICE DEPARTMENT AT APPROXIMATELY 9:00 PM LAST NIGHT AFTER NOTICING THE VICTIM'S VEHICLE ABANDONED IN FRONT OF THE WAREHOUSE.

AFTER FURTHER SURVEYAL, THE OFFICER NOTICED MR. MITCHELL'S BODY LYING INSIDE OF THE WAREHOUSE IN AN OPEN SPACE IN A FETAL POSITION WITH MULTIPLE BULLET WOUNDS TO HIS BODY AND HEAD. THE HYATTSVILLE P.D. POLICE CHIEF SAID THAT THEY HAVE NO SUSPECTS OF INTEREST AT THE TIME, BUT THEY DO BELIEVE THIS INCIDENT WAS DRUG RELATED...

After I hit the power button on the television, I climbed out of bed, grabbed my phone and called Little Bo. I wanted to check up on him to make sure that he was doing okay and to let him know that I loved him. It's been three days since I killed Big Mike and to tell you the truth, I feel a lot better about life than I did before his death.

I guess it's because I've finally got closure. Sonya's been calling Tanya and me frequently for the past two days asking if we heard from Big Mike. We gave her the same answer, "No Sonya, but you'll be the first to know if we do." Later during the day, Sonya made sure that we were the first to know when she called crying about Big Mike's murder.

I played the situation cool and acted surprised as if I never knew. After my five star Oscar performance, I passed the phone to Tanya so that she could do what women do during rough times, console! Tanya assisted Sonya in preparing the funeral arrangements in which about 15 people showed up. Throughout the whole ordeal, Tanya and Sonya became best buddies and they talked to each other daily.

They attended church together, went to the spa, nail salon, beauty parlor, clothes shopping and wherever else they could think of going together. I waited until I got rid of all of my product I had in the streets before I re'd up. I counted all of my money out and estimated my goals. I then tripled my orders and let Jay and Marty know that this was my last trip, and that I was retiring from a life of crime.

I also informed them about my business plans, which drew interest from the both of them. Together, we opened, CLEAN CUT GROOMING CENTER.

We started out with three locations, one in D.C., one in Baltimore,

Maryland, and one in Charlotte, North Carolina, with plans to expand

nationwide, thanks to a business plan that secured a hefty business

loan. Together, Tanya and I are the majority owners, benefiting from

60% of the company while Jay and Marty are the minority owners,

benefiting from 20% a piece. I also took a page out of Fahmi and

Cold Billy's success manuscript and started my own non-profit

organization. It's called CON-WAY.

I put it together with the help of Tanya. Con-Way was an

organization that helped ex-convicts re-enter themselves back into

society after serving an extended prison sentence of at least 10 years.

We provide temporary housing and help ex-cons find stable

employment before being released from our program. Mental

counseling as well as family counseling is also provided. The program

is a 6 to 18 month program. I also inherited my cousin Vell's vehicle

towing service as well as his boxing gym. I changed the name from

Round 1 Boxing, to BoVell's Boxing. Tanya and I finally got married

the following spring, on Tanya's birthday, April 1st.

One month later, Sonya remarried another convict she met on a website called writeaprisoner.com. For her to be such a beautiful and successful woman, she sure did love the bad guy type. I guess in some cases, opposites do attract.

Tanya and I gave up the apartment life for good and dragged Little Bo into a four bedroom, two and one half bath single family home with a basement and two car garage in Fort Washington, Maryland. "Just a few minutes away from **MGM Grand Casino and Resort**" is what the realtor kept stressing. She explained to us how the area was a great place to raise a family due to the lack of gun violence. She let us know that she had a 22 year old son whose dad was murdered before his birth in the '90s. Tanya thought that she was flirting because of how she kept referring to my eyes as familiar looking. When I told her my age, that's when she realized that she didn't know me.

She was a nice lady. If I'm not mistaken, I think she said her name was Stacy. Stacy Peterson, that is. The police once questioned me about Big Mike's death. They said that I was the last outgoing call on his call log. I told them that that was the last time we talked and that, "he said something about meeting with his money train, whatever that meant?"

They later had a warrant signed by a judge to check my cell phone tower records, to see my whereabouts from the day that Big Mike died until he was discovered by the police. Thanks to Wee-Wee chasing that '88 crack, which she never found, the cell phone tower records showed my phone bouncing off of every tower in the Cruddy Island community.

There was no motive that supported their speculation as well as no physical evidence, so they fell back. No witness, no weapon, no case. The only person that can convict me is me, and I'll be damned if I pull a G. Dep and give the police a special delivery.

Fuck my conscience, I enjoy freedom. Throughout time, I became a firm believer of "everything happens for a reason. I mean, I would probably still be in the drug trade had I not caught that gun and marijuana case. I probably would have never acted on changing my life for the better versus talking about it.

And yes, 2PAC said, "Revenge is like the sweetest joy next to getting pussy," but he did also say, "We must remember that tomorrow comes after the dark," and my tomorrow became my today. Though I became a little anti-social after this crazy and twisted situation, I still had some friends.

I remember back in my crack selling days, a wise fiend named Uncle Polo said to me, "Louis! These niggaz ain't scared to die, they just scared to live. They so ready to go, but not ready to grow. Change the trend, Lou. You special!"

To this day, those words beat through my brain like a headache. I'm trying to live and grow for the sake of Tanya and Little Bo. So every day when I wake I pray, "God, protect me from my friends 'cause I can handle my enemies."

See, in life, you can never 100% predict the next man's intentions.

People have motives and hidden agendas, but I learned to accept that

in life. Which takes me back to that little boy sitting Indian-style and

eating popcorn while sitting in front of my mother's television

watching the Forrest Gump movie. Forrest said, "Life is like a box of

chocolates... you never know what 'cha gonna get."

Well Forrest, I got a peace. Peace!

THE END